OUTBACK RUNAWAY

Running away from the heartbreak of a disastrous love affair, Dale headed for the outback, and the Vining family who had been her refuge from unhappiness years ago. But all she found was Trelawney Saber, with a bracingly unsympathetic attitude to her troubles!

Books you will enjoy
by DOROTHY CORK

THE KURRANULLA ROUND

Matty was in North-West Australia to see how her dear Uncle Jerry was getting on—and found that the one thing Uncle Jerry wanted was to see her safely married, if possible to Dirk Reasoner. But Matty knew something her uncle didn't—and that was the reason why Dirk would never trust or respect her, let alone love her . . .

WALKABOUT WIFE

No one wanted to marry Edie—they wanted other things, but not marriage! So in a fit of pique she answered an advert: 'Cattleman seeks wife, preferably under thirty-five'. The cattleman in question turned out to be Drew Sutton—and eligibility was his middle name. There had to be a snag somewhere, Edie thought. There was . . .

ISLAND OF ESCAPE

It was because she felt sorry for her flighty cousin Jan's treatment of her sheep-farmer fiancé—and because Jan had stolen her own boy-friend Paul—that Ellis wrote to the sheep-farmer suggesting they console each other. What Ellis had in mind was helping him on the sheep station or something useful like that, but it seemed he had completely misunderstood her . . .

FORGET AND FORGIVE

'French and English just don't mix,' thought Brianna—with some justification, for her English father and French mother had split up years ago. Nevertheless, she now felt it was time to visit her mother in France and forget the bitterness of the past. And so she might have done, if it had not been for her uncompromising French stepbrother Philippe!

OUTBACK RUNAWAY

BY

DOROTHY CORK

MILLS & BOON LIMITED
LONDON W1

First published 1980
Australian copyright 1980
Philippine copyright 1980
This edition 1980

© Dorothy Cork 1980

ISBN 0 263 73298 3

Set in Linotype Plantin

*Made and printed in Great Britain
by Richard Clay (The Chaucer Press), Ltd.,
Bungay, Suffolk*

CHAPTER ONE

THE dark had come quickly. For the last little while, the headlights of Dale Driscoll's car had picked out nothing more than spinifex and gidgee, stretching away into nothingness at either side of the rutted track that was the back way into Jackalass. With so much monotony, it wasn't until she saw the thick dark line of trees marking the watercourse that she knew how close she was to the end of her journey. Another fifteen minutes and she would be there.

Shortly after, the Torana went plunging down the bank and splashed through the shallow water of the creek. It was very different, she reflected, from when she had left Jackalass ten years ago. Then, it was the Wet and the floods had come, so that the waters of the big lagoon had spread up and up until they reached the lower rooms of the homestead. But this was only late October. The Wet was weeks and weeks ahead.

Her foot hard on the accelerator, she drove up the other side of the creek and through the trees, curved left with the wheel-tracks, and stared ahead into the darkness, looking for the homestead lights. She could see a flicker of flame among the trees, smell the smoke of a fire, and she knew it was from the Aborigines' camp. Not a light showed anywhere else, though the illuminated dial of her wristwatch put the time at only ten minutes to nine.

Dale was mystified. It was too early for everyone to have gone to bed. Even if the men were out at the muster camp, getting ready for the big December cattle sales, someone

5

would be at home. Aunt Beth—the cook, Mrs Miller—some of the girls——

'I should have let them know I was coming,' she thought uneasily. Last summer she hadn't even sent her usual Christmas letter to the Vinings at Jackalass. Her mind had been too full of Andrew MacWade. And the fact was, she was now right out of touch.

All the same, Aunt Beth had assured her many times, 'Come and stay with us whenever you like. You'll always be welcome.' And when Beth Vining said a thing, she really meant it. So everything was going to be all right, Dale comforted herself.

Yet *something* was wrong, she realised, as she drove up the slight rise and reached the home paddock. There was not a glimmer of light, not even from the big kitchen block that was linked to the house by a covered way.

She parked the car by the stores and leaned into the back for her suitcase. As she climbed out of the car she heard the faint hum of the electricity generator and the crowing of a rooster from the poultry yard beyond the garden. She was reassured. Of course someone was home! Aunt Beth must have gone early to bed. She walked on towards the two-storied homestead on its tall wooden piles, wondering which of the Vinings still lived at home, whether Kevin and young David were working on the property with their father. Joanna would still be away at school, and Rebie—twenty-two now, a year older than Dale herself—had never been an outdoor girl. She was probably living in Brisbane. But Buff had always loved the outback. Surely she'd be here, particularly as Aunt Beth hadn't been terribly strong.

The house was dark and the silence somehow eerie. Dale felt her way past the canvas chairs that had always stood in the shade of the big mango trees, and brushed away a mosquito that was buzzing in her hair. When she pulled tentatively at the wire screen door that led into the living room, it opened. She stepped inside and groped for the light switch. It was funny how certain things could be etched so ineradicably on one's mind. She knew exactly where she'd find the light switch, and now, as she blinked in the light and looked around her, she discovered the room looked familiar and yet different, as if it had grown away from her, or she from it. It had been redecorated, not surprisingly, though the concrete floor, the cane furniture, the big dining table and chairs at the far side of the room were unchanged. But now, instead of the old cream-painted split cane blinds, there were curtains, ivory-coloured with a big splashed-on pattern of green leaves. The green cushions on the chair were new too, and Dale wondered who had chosen the fabrics. *That* made her think with a sharp spasm of pain of Andrew—who until five days ago had been her boss in the furniture and decoration shop in Rockhampton.

Oh God! She suddenly set down her suitcase on the floor, overcome by a feeling that was near panic. This was all turning out so differently from how she had imagined it. Family, she'd thought. A welcoming family, though Beth and David were only courtesy aunt and uncle. Surprise—excitement—warmth and talk. Eager chatter about what everyone had been doing, while they made a big pot of tea and cooked up something simple like scrambled eggs in the little kitchen. And Dale would explain why she'd arrived so late. She'd been on the road two and a half days, making early morning starts, and this afternoon she'd simply had to pull off the road and have a sleep. Then before she went to bed, she'd imagined herself telling Aunt Beth about Andrew, having a good cry. And being comforted. The way she'd comforted her when she was nine and her father was marrying again, and they'd wanted her out of the way.

'You'll have a lovely, lovely time with us, darling,' Aunt Beth had said, in such a warm motherly way, though she'd never met Dale until that day. 'When you go back they'll be so happy to see you, and you'll have such lots to tell them. You'll see—it will all come right.'

For Dale, it had been a disaster period, the crumbling of her world. She was in a similar situation now, she had the same need of comfort. She felt the tears running down her cheeks, felt her lips grow warm and tremble. Where was Aunt Beth?

'Oh, please——' she said weakly against the shaking fingers she had put to her mouth.

Her voice sounded odd and unreal in the silence of the house. Where was everybody? Hadn't anyone heard her come in—seen the light? There had to be *someone*—with the generator going. And besides, she suddenly realised, there was a teacup on the dining room table.

She left her suitcase on the floor where she'd dropped it and went to the stairs that led up to the bedrooms. At the top of the stairs was a wide verandah that was used as a sleep-out when the nights were too humid to use the bedrooms. Dale stopped there, put on the light, and called softly, 'Aunt Beth?' No one answered, and after a moment she began to move quietly along the verandah, pausing to listen at each of the bedroom doors, sure somehow that there was no one there, yet knowing there had to be.

There was.

As she reached the bedroom furthest from the stairs, she could hear breathing. And she could smell whisky. Very strongly. It couldn't be Aunt Beth, so who was it? Her mind flipped anxiously over each member of the Vining family, rejecting them all in turn. Not one of them, she was positive, would be filling himself—or herself—up with whisky. She thought too of the governess, Arnoldine Bell, and then of Trelawney Saber, the grandson of the owner of this big cattle station, of which Jackalass was the out-station. *He* had been sent away from Jackalass—but it hadn't been for heavy drinking.

Dale said into the warm darkness of the room, 'Who's there? Are you awake?' Her voice wavered slightly, and when there was no reply she resolutely, yet a little fear-fully, switched on the light—and smothered a gasp.

The man sprawled in sleep on top of the disordered bed *was* Trelawney Saber.

Her recognition of him was instant, and it was shocked. She stood motionless, her heart beating fast.

He was fully dressed except that his feet were bare, and his tan and cream striped shirt had come adrift from dark, narrow-legged pants that were impregnated with dust. He didn't stir, though the room was flooded with light. He was deeply, heavily asleep, and Dale's glance took in the glass and the half empty whisky bottle that stood on the chest by the bed, before returning to him. His face looked drawn and haggard, and to Dale he seemed to have grown older by more than the ten years or so that had passed since last she saw him. He must be still in his early thirties, but he looked years older. The result of hard drinking? she won-dered, something within her deeply disturbed.

Her eyes wandered over the thick tawny hair that fell rough and tangled across his tanned forehead, giving the impression that fingers had been raked through it rather than that it had been combed. She moved a little closer, leaned down and said distinctly, 'Trelawney——'

He didn't open his eyes, but he moved sharply and his forehead creased. He muttered a word she'd sooner not have heard, then expelled his whisky-laden breath on a long groan.

Dale straightened up with a feeling of nausea. She would never have dreamed that he would take to drink, no matter what his other sins. And they, as far as she knew, were mainly connected with women. When she'd first come to Jackalass, he was working for Ray Saber, his uncle, at Warathar, the home station, though he had occasionally visited Jackalass. At first Dale had thought it was to see Buff, who'd been home for the school holidays and was obviously in love with him. Later, she'd discovered it was to see the pretty, dark-haired governess, Arnoldine Bell. He'd go for picnics with them, help the children build dams in the creek, talk to them about the bush, find wierd lizards, birds' nests, snake tracks—even snakes. He had made picnic days exciting, and it had been a shock to Dale to happen on the wild side of his nature—the womanising side. It was Rebie who somehow found out the reason why he finally left Warathar and came to work on Jackalass: He had been 'kissing' Stephanie, the girl Ray Saber was about to marry.

'And do you know why his grandfather sent him outback to begin with?' Rebie had asked Dale, her short-sighted eyes wide and excited behind her glasses. 'He had an *affair* with a girl whose father works on the stud farm!'

By the time it happened Dale hadn't been in the least surprised that Trelawney was leaving Jackalass. She didn't imagine Uncle David would want him around, the havoc he was causing. She'd often wondered what had happened to him. She'd imagined he'd find work on some other cattle station on the Gulf country, but that he should have turned into a drunk was very hard to take. Perhaps oddly, she felt bitterly disappointed in him, and before she left the room she reached out and commandeered the whisky bottle. He wasn't going to drink any more tonight . . .

What was she going to do now? The idea of sleeping up here had become quite impossible. The wild Trelawney she remembered was bad enough, but the man he had become was far worse. The further she could get away from him the better.

Badly shaken, she left the room, switching off the light after her, then making her way downstairs again. The cook —Mrs Miller, she thought hopefully, as she deposited the whisky bottle on the dining room table. She crossed the room and went along the covered way towards the kitchen. Remembered scents drifted to her nostrils—cedar flowers, oleanders—but she scarcely noticed them, her mind was too occupied with her dilemma. She knew in her heart, before she even looked into the big room next to the kitchen, that Mrs Miller wouldn't be there. No one answered when she knocked, and she opened the door and went inside. Plainly, Mrs Miller didn't live here any more. No one did. The room that had been both bedroom and private sitting room to the cook had been turned into a utility room. There was a sewing machine, a work table, an ironing board. A sturdy writing desk had a row of books on it, and there were two straight-backed chairs and an armchair. Dale sank down in the armchair, avoiding the reflection of her black-clad figure in the long wall mirror that had always been there.

She didn't know what to do, whether to cry or to get back into her car and drive away. The trouble was, where to? Besides, it didn't make sense, after coming all this long way, simply to go without even finding out where everyone was first. Suddenly it occurred to her that they could be visiting another station, staying the night. Of course! That must be it. There might be a wedding—picnic races— some sort of celebration. Damn Trelawney Saber! If he had to be here, couldn't he be sober, and able to explain it all to her? Maybe they were all over at Warathar, visiting Ray Saber, and that could account for Trelawney not being with them, even if it didn't account for his being here.

Anyway, what was she going to do?

She looked thoughtfully around the room. She could make up a bed here, bring a mattress and bedclothes over from the house, lock the door, sleep on the floor. What a fool she'd been not to let them know she was coming! Then there'd surely have been someone to meet her. But she'd been in such a state over Andrew, she'd hardly known what she was doing. She reined in her thoughts sharply. She mustn't start thinking about Andrew. She'd sleep here, and with that decided, she headed for the little kitchen at the back of the main house, the kitchen the family had always used. In the fridge there were milk and eggs and fresh meat, and she drank half a glass of the creamy milk, then put two eggs on the table ready to cook after she'd been upstairs, and fixed her bed.

Upstairs, she decided not to raid the bedrooms. There were several stretchers on the verandah, and she took a mattress and pillow from one of them and lugged it to the top of the stairs. From the linen cupboard there she took two sheets, a pillow slip, a cotton blanket, and a bath towel. By then she had quite a load and she wondered if she'd manage to get it all down the stairs in one go, without an accident. She stood where she was for a moment, listening intently. She could hear quite distinctly the sound of Trelawney Saber's breathing, and felt infuriated with him for being asleep. He could have helped her with these things, she thought—illogically, because actually she didn't want him staggering out here, breathing whisky fumes and making a nuisance of himself. The most sensible thing to do was to make two trips.

She took the mattress down first. It was kapok-filled and awkward, because it was too thick to roll up, but she managed. Then she went back for the bedclothes, pausing to hear again the steady sound of breathing. She made a slight grimace. He was sleeping it off, all right. He'd have a sore head in the morning. Andrew had never drunk too much.

Dale switched her thoughts back to more practical matters, and once everything she needed was downstairs she transported it, plus her suitcase, out to Mrs Miller's room. She fixed up her bed on the floor, laid out her pyjamas, her brush and comb, her toothpaste and soap. Then she set off for the little kitchen to cook scrambled eggs.

There was no bread. Mrs Miller used to make about twenty loaves every second day, but Mrs Miller wasn't here now, and it didn't look as though she'd been replaced. Dale found some dry biscuits to eat with her eggs. She wasn't really hungry, but if she didn't eat, she probably wouldn't sleep, and having cooked the eggs, she forced them down. She drank some more milk, washed up her things and tidied them away, reflecting that the kitchen was far from being as spick and span as Aunt Beth used always to keep it. Then she made her way back to the bed she'd prepared for herself.

She wondered if the cowboy might wake and see her light through the trees and come and investigate. In case that should happen, she decided to undress in the small downstairs shower room.

Ten minutes later she was in her pyjamas and all but ready for bed, the black sleeveless vest and black jeans she'd been wearing laid carefully over the back of one of the chairs. From habit, she took up her brush and brushed her hair before getting into bed. From habit, she stood in

front of the mirror to do it. Heavens, what a sight she
looked! Her face pale and tired and washed out above the
pale creamy-coloured pyjamas, her blonde hair short and
unfamiliar and unflattering. She'd had it cut yesterday in
some little town whose name she couldn't even remember.
Very badly cut, she saw now. It was certainly cool, but it
looked frightful, and she brushed it back almost savagely
from the smoothness of her forehead. Aunt Beth would
have a fit to see her, she thought, her soft mouth drooping
with tiredness. She felt she hadn't smiled for centuries.
There hadn't been all that much to smile about, lately; not
since her love affair with Andrew MacWade had come to a
very bitter end. Staring, unseeingly now, at her reflection,
and brushing her hair mechanically, she let the whole saga
slide unchecked through her mind.

It had started in earnest when her father decided to
leave Gladstone and move south to Brisbane. Dale hadn't
wanted to go, and her father hadn't insisted, though Olivia
—her stepmother—was piqued at losing her help with the
children. But her father had conceded, 'You have your
own life to live, darling,' and he'd let her have Olivia's old
car, the Torana, because Olivia would be getting a new one
in Brisbane.

So Dale too had packed up and moved, but north, to
Rockhampton and for a reason she kept to herself. The
fact was, Andrew MacWade was there. Until three months
previously he'd been working in the MacWade furnishing
shop in Gladstone—which was where Dale worked too—
but he'd been sent to manage the Rockhampton branch,
and Dale had been shattered. The absurd thing was, though
she had fallen desperately, romantically, in love with him,
he didn't even know she existed. But she couldn't free her
mind of him, didn't want to. Other men didn't interest her,
and when she found her employers were prepared to let her

work in Rockhampton she was madly excited.

She'd soon set herself up in a flat with a girl called Sally Hayman, and soon too, the bubble of her elation had burst. She'd daydreamed wildly of all the fantastic things that might happen when she met Andrew again, but none of them did. He remembered her, but barely, and that was all. Dale was in despair until, unwittingly, Sally came to her aid. Sally was the complete opposite of the innocent and inexperienced Dale, who hadn't the slightest idea as to how to go about attracting a man. Sally had lashings of boyfriends whom she appeared to attract with no effort at all.

It was a combination of looks, clothes, manner, Dale decided after some time. Plus of course the intrinsic factor that was personality and about which she could do nothing. But she could do something about the other factors and Sally, being a beautician and seeing Dale experimenting, was generous with her help. Dale had soon given her soft corn-coloured hair a lift with the use of a saucy coppery rinse, and she became expert with sophisticated make-up. Meticulously and thoroughly she changed her style of dressing. That had cost her a packet, all she could afford each payday for weeks and weeks. But it had results. Andrew began to notice her—really notice her—and as a final touch, Dale adopted some of Sally's little mannerisms. She developed a technique, whenever Andrew had occasion to speak to her, of softening her lips, parting them slightly, and looking straight into his eyes. Then after a moment she'd drop her gaze fractionally before looking up at him again. It was shameless in a way, and she was aware that it was an invitation, but it worked amazingly.

Andrew began to take her with him to the homes of various clients, where he would discuss decor, colour schemes, fabrics with her. It certainly gave her career and her self-confidence a boost, and she blossomed as she had never done before. Her relationship with Andrew raced ahead with a speed that had her in a daze. All the things she had merely dreamed about for so long actually began to happen. He took her out to dinner, to shows and to concerts. Week ends they went to the disco or over to the Capricorn Coast. There were kisses, caresses, and it was all unbelievably thrilling, a dream come true.

All the same, she was taken by surprise when he wanted to make love to her. She just wasn't ready for that. When she'd daydreamed about that sort of thing, they'd been married, and Andrew hadn't yet asked her to marry him. She knew it was unkind to lead a man on and then to say no, so she used her head and her ingenuity to avoid getting into situations where they were so alone he might be tempted to make love to her. It wasn't easy, but she promised herself it wouldn't be for long. She was as certain as that that he wanted to marry her.

Then suddenly, without any warning at all, the whole thing ended.

Andrew went to Brisbane on a business trip and when he came back, he'd simply dropped her, completely and unmistakably. Dale couldn't believe it. She was nearly out of her mind with despair and bewilderment. To be greeted each day with a cool nod, a token smile, and after that, ignored—it just couldn't be true. And when, in her despair, she followed him to his office and asked him tearfully, pathetically, 'Andrew—*why*?' he answered her callously,

'I guess cold-blooded girls are not to my taste, that's all.'

Cold-blooded!

'But, Andrew,' she had faltered, 'don't you see—it was only because—it wouldn't be like that when we were *married*.'

He'd turned away from her. 'Look, it's all over, Dale. I've got myself another girl-friend and I'm not open to negotiation. Why don't you find someone your own age so you can do your growing up together?'

She had stared at him, speechless and stunned. Bang!—you're dead. Just like that. One shot. Then she had turned blindly away and gone back to the shop.

The next day she saw him with his new girl-friend, and knew that he'd meant her to. She'd never known jealousy could be so painful, and it taught her that she couldn't stay on. She just wasn't a strong enough character to stand up to seeing him every day and being ignored. Time was said to heal all wounds, but if the wound is continually being prodded, reopened, then time can be a very slow healer.

Dale made up her mind one miserable sleepless night that she'd leave Rockhampton. But to go where? Not to Brisbane, not back to babysitting for Olivia; she'd grown too used to her independence for that. Then out of the blue had come the brilliant idea of retreating to Jackalass, to Aunt Beth and the Vinings, and a state of uncomplicated innocence. Far from the adult world of sexual love and heartache and jealousy. The relief there was in the very thought of it! Never again, she promised herself, would she set out deliberately to attract a man. She'd be plain asexual Dale Driscoll again, the girl men simply didn't notice...

Dale laid down her hairbrush and focussed sombrely on her reflection. Her gold-flecked hazel eyes stared back at her. They looked centuries old, she thought, though certainly they were the only thing about her that *did* look old. She'd sought sanctuary, she reflected, but she hadn't found it yet. She'd arrived at Jackalass, but she felt neither safe nor at peace. Not by any means.

Something moved in the mirror. The door, that had proved to have no lock, was opening. The cowboy, she thought, her heart hammering. He must have seen the light.

She spun round, ready to explain.

But it wasn't the cowboy. It was Trelawney Saber who pushed the door wide open and, leaning against the frame, stared across at her through narrowed blue eyes that were more green than blue. His shirt hung untidily outside the waistband of his dark pants, and his face looked strained and grey under its deep tan. Which was not surprising, Dale thought, distastefully aware of the reek of whisky. Briefly she wondered if she should feel sorry for him, but she didn't, couldn't. Trelawney Saber just wasn't the sort of man you could feel sorry for.

For perhaps a minute neither of them spoke. Dale's throat was dry, constricted. She wanted badly to say something authoritative and full of self-confidence. Something like, 'I suppose you've been looking for your whisky bottle.' Or, 'Why don't you go back to bed and go to sleep?' Yet she could say nothing, and she stood trembling inwardly while he looked her over, his long blue-green eyes finally coming back to her face.

'My—God!' he said then, slowly and not very clearly. 'I do believe it's little Daisy Driscoll! For a moment I thought it was going to be Rebie messing around out here.'

'Rebie?' Dale echoed faintly. His calling her Daisy had somehow unnerved her. Nobody called her Daisy these days. Nobody had since she'd left Jackalass. 'Is Rebie here?'

He had moved away from the door frame to come right into the room, and he was still staring at her. Dale breathed deeply and stayed where she was, her back to the mirror, trying to assure herself that she could handle him all right. She knew he was wild, she knew what he was like with women—how he'd played around with Stephanie, and Arnoldine Bell, and heaven knew who else. But she was only 'little Daisy Driscoll'. And the mirror had told her only minutes ago what a fright she looked with her badly cut hair and her pallid face. He'd never in a fit be attracted by her, thank goodness.

'Well?' she repeated with little more confidence. '*Is* Rebie here?'

He halted a few feet from her and raised a hand to rake his fingers through already untidy hair. He had highish cheekbones, and her gaze was drawn to the long crease in one of his lean cheeks—a crease that looked like a deep laughter line but was actually a scar.

'I reckon she's not back yet,' he said at last, his voice still blurred. 'But how the hell do you come to be here, prowling about the house at this hour of night? And what's this in aid of?' he concluded, kicking the edge of the mattress with his bare foot.

Dale swallowed. 'It's for me to sleep on,' she said shortly.

His right eyebrow—the one that had the peak in it— rose a fraction. 'Uncommunicative, aren't you? Why didn't you let someone know you were coming? You didn't, did you?'

'There wasn't time,' she said defensively.

'There's a telephone,' he said with the suggestion of a smile. 'So what was the great big hurry? Another disaster period in your life?'

She flinched as though he had flicked her on a raw place —as he had—and asked defensively, 'What do you mean?'

'Oh, you know what I mean, Daisy,' he said wearily. 'We'll go into it some other time if you like, but not just now. You may have forgotten, but I was here the first couple of days when you turned up as a kid. You don't look to have grown up much since then, by the way. Still as if you've been whipped emotionally—and recently. Is it stepmother trouble that's made you go bush?'

Dale didn't answer. She changed the subject. 'Where is everyone, anyhow?'

'At the muster camp.'

'Not Aunt Beth too!' she exclaimed in surprise, and felt his glance sharpen, as if his senses had suddenly become more alert.

'Beth? You don't know——' He broke off and began again. 'How long is it since you were in touch, Daisy?'

The question made her feel guilty, and she told him reluctantly but vaguely, 'It's quite a while. I haven't written since I changed my address and moved to Rockhampton. But Aunt Beth always said I could come here any time I wanted.' She stopped on the point of protesting further. It had nothing to do with Trelawney Saber, even if his grandfather did own the station. *He* wasn't boss here. Or—or was he? She suddenly realised that things could have changed, and a feeling of sick nervousness welled up in her.

He moved closer and looked down at her, and she was aware of his height, of the broadness of his shoulders. Somewhere at the back of her mind a picture formed of him and Arnoldine—and she wondered if he was married.

'A lot of water's flowed under the bridge in the last little while,' he said slowly. 'How about coming along to the kitchen and brewing some tea, and we can talk about it.'

'About—what?' Now he was so close to her, she could see he was sweating slightly, and the whisky fumes on his breath made her nostrils dilate, and she moved away from him. 'You can—we can talk in the morning. You'd better go back to bed.'

He stared at her and then laughed shortly. 'You think I've been boozing up, don't you, little Daisy Driscoll?'

'I know you have,' she said, feeling a little angry. He spoke as if she were a fool. 'And don't keep calling me that. I'm twenty-one.'

'You are?' he exclaimed, and his eyes went quickly to her

breast, its shape visible, but not outlined, under the loose cotton pyjama top, then roamed down the length of her and came back to her face. 'Well, you could have fooled me. You look about fifteen, and you're acting as if you were twelve. What have you been doing with yourself all these years, in Rockhampton or wherever?'

'It doesn't matter what I've been doing,' Dale retorted. 'Just leave me alone, and go back to bed. I'm tired—I've been driving for days——'

'Then you're probably *over*-tired. All churned up and wondering about everyone too. Well, my guess is that neither of us will sleep if we get back to bed now, so we might as well talk. There are things you'll have to know.'

'What things?' Dale asked uncertainly. 'Why can't you tell me now and be done with it?'

'Because I don't choose to rush it. And if you think in your chaste little heart that I'm drunk—and dangerous—forget it. Drunk I may be, but dangerous, no. You're safe with me tonight, Daisy.' He was unbuttoning his shirt as he spoke, and Dale watched, her pulses racing. What could she do—alone with a man like Trelawney Saber? Run screaming into the darkness? Enlist the aid of the cowboy? She couldn't see it. But what else was there to do?

Then her eyes opened wide. Under the shirt, Trelawney Saber's chest was encased in what looked like a broad elastic belt.

'What you're gaping at is a rib belt, Daisy,' he said. 'I cracked a couple of ribs at the muster today. By the time I'd ridden the considerable distance here, and fixed myself up in this thing, I tell you I was in need of something to put me to sleep. And my choice, though I agree it may not have been yours, was whisky.'

Dale's lips had parted soundlessly. So that was wh[...] looked so strained and haggard. He was hurt—a[...]

been so censorious. She felt both guilt and compassion, and at another level, a deep relief. It had gone very much against the grain somehow to accept that Trelawney had turned into a drunkard.

It was the relief that made her eyes flood with sudden tears, and she recoiled when he said harshly, 'And now you can forget it. I'm not in need of tears or of ministrations. I can look after myself very adequately, and right now I'm as comfortable as can be expected. So let's get that cup of tea.'

Dale knew she was going to have to give in. But he looked so uncivilised with his messed-up hair, his haggard face, his unbuttoned shirt, and she was very conscious that she was wearing nothing but a pair of sleeveless cotton pyjamas. Yet he couldn't be very dangerous with cracked ribs. Moreover, she had a nervous feeling that he had something bad to tell her, and she knew he was right. If she went to bed now she wouldn't sleep; she'd lie awake wondering what it was all about.

'All right.' She went ahead of him to the little kitchen. She put the water on and found the teapot and tea caddy while he set out two mugs, then disappeared into the living room. He came back just as she'd made the tea, and he had the whisky bottle with him.

'What's that for?' she asked aggressively.

'You're going to have a dash of it in your tea.'

Her heart seemed to stop fractionally. So it must be bad news.

─── of them spoke again until she'd poured the tea,
        ─teaming, into the mugs. Trelawney took the top
             bottle and Dale said petulantly, 'I don't want
              ─ her and splashed a generous amount into

It was a command and she found herself obeying it. The tea was very hot and the whisky gave it a slightly sweetish taste. It burned on her palate and on her throat, warmed her and stimulated her. She drank it more quickly than she was used to drinking anything hot, and in fact she set her mug down no more than a second after Trelawney. It occurred to her that her father would have a fit if he could have seen good Scotch being splashed recklessly into mugs of tea in an outback kitchen. The thought made her want to laugh, and the man sitting at the table with her frowned.

'If you'd arrived a couple of days ago,' he said presently, 'you'd have found Rebecca here. She's gone out to the muster with a couple of folks who've come over from Brisbane for a holiday and want to see how the bushies live.'

'Oh, has she?' Dale said inadequately. So Rebie still lived here—'And the others?' she asked, as he reached for the teapot.

'The others. Well, things have changed,' he said, his voice hard. Deliberately hard, she thought, and she felt herself tense for what was coming—suspected something like it even before it came. 'Kevin's managing the outstation now. Beth hadn't been well, and David finally bought a small property near Charters Towers. The climate's good there, but——' He had lowered his eyes and now he raised them and looked straight at her, and she looked back at him, her breathing constricted. 'Nothing could prevent what had to happen. Beth died three months ago.'

Dale said nothing. She raised her mug and swa[llowed] some of the tea he had just poured for her. So [Beth] was gone. She'd never see her again. The woma[n who had] been aunt—or mother—to her for two an[d] when she had badly needed someone woman whose kindness and warmth she would never forget. It was bitter to realise she had lost touch so carelessly, hadn't let the Vinings know she'd left Gladstone, hadn't even sent her usual Christmas greeting—and all because of her self-absorption. She wanted to cry, but tears are useless, and instead she sat, eyes downcast, twisting the mug endlessly between her hands, struggling for control.

'Finish your tea,' said Trelawney, then went on talking. 'Buff went over to look after her father—she's still there. She'd been keeping house for Kevin, but Rebie's doing that now. In her fashion ... As for the others, young David's studying to be a musician, and Joanne's at boarding school in Charters Towers. I think that just about brings you up to date with what's happening in the Vining family.'

'Yes.' Dale's tears were under control now, and she asked him, more to show that she wasn't going to break down than for any other reason, 'And what about you? What are you doing here?'

'Me?' She didn't glance up, but she could feel him looking at her broodingly from under his brows. 'Well, I'm the boss around here these days. The old man—my grandfather—died. He left Ray the stud farm down south, and Warathar to me.'

'Then why are you here—at Jackalass? I mean, Kevin's ᵉ manager here—you said so.' At last she dared to look ᵐ and suprised him with a twist of pain on his mouth, ᵗ suddenly she realised his chest must be hurting.

ᵉ on a visit,' he said dryly. 'Part business, part had one of my stockmen drive me over from is morning. I wanted to meet the Richards, ree days, do a bit of socialising and have a tomorrow, about the sales. Then the damned horse racked my ribs. Rebecca will be back he has some sewing she wants to do at Warathar. We're redecorating over there.'

Dale blinked. Rebie doing sewing, helping with Warathar's redecoration? Rebie—who'd never cared for domestic tasks but liked to listen to the radio, to gossip, to speculate, and always looked so wise, so old for her years as she did it, with her round face and her spectacles. Anyhow, there was a sewing machine in Mrs Miller's old room. Couldn't she make curtains or whatever it was out there, instead of going all the way to Warathar?

With a feeling of weariness Dale realised she had landed herself head first among a group of people she didn't know any more. Aunt Beth would have still been the same, and it had been Aunt Beth she'd been looking for—Aunt Beth and her own childhood. And both of them were gone. She felt tired and confused, and that, she thought, finishing her tea, must be due to the whisky she had drunk. It would help her sleep anyhow, and tomorrow Rebie would be back. Everything would be a little more normal, though it could never be as she had imagined. There was just one other person she had to ask about, and that was Arnoldine Bell. She knew that when Joanne had gone away to boarding school Arnoldine had stayed on to help Beth, but she hadn't known that Beth's health had been in such a bad state as it must have been.

'Arnoldine,' she asked Trelawney. 'Where's she these days?'

'She's over at Warathar.'

Her eyes widened. 'You—you're married?' she stammered, wondering why she hadn't considered that p[...]bility before.

'What? To Arnoldine? Good God, no!' H[...] curved in a very masculine, very sophisticated, shock—'She's just—looking after me.'

Looking after him! In what way? she [...]

ing herself slightly. A confusion of images and emotions
and thoughts jostled against each other in her head. Trelawney and Arnoldine that evening among the orange trees
—the scent of orange blossoms—the molten gold of the
moon against the darkly hot outback sky. The passionate
kisses Trelawney had been planting on the governess's
throat, her little cries—Dale had run away from the scene
shocked and disturbed. It wasn't only what she had seen;
it was, as well, because she knew Buff was in love with him.
Later, he was banished from Jackalass—for seducing the
governess, Rebie had said, though at that stage of her life
Dale had been far from sure what that meant. And Buff
had cried and cried.

So she knew, really, what Arnie's 'looking after' was
likely to mean. She wasn't a child now, she knew something of human passion, even though she hadn't experienced it to the full herself—and through refusing, had
lost Andrew ...

She got unsteadily to her feet. 'Is there anything I can
do for you before I go to bed, Trelawney?'

'Not a thing.' He was looking at her searchingly, and
strangely he didn't seem the least bit drunk now. Dale was
the one who felt intoxicated and was aware, whether he
was or not, of the slight slur in her speech. 'Are you all
ight, Daisy? I know you've taken a knock. The whisky
uld help you sleep.'

uess it will.' She tried to smile but couldn't. 'I'm all

you ined to stick to the outside room and sleep on
'I'There are plenty of comfortable beds upstairs,
said aloo

'I'll try no up in Mrs Miller's room, thank you,' she
t worry about me.'

e said dryly. 'Well, goodnight, Daisy.

We'll meet again in the morning.' He got up from his chair and was gone.

Dale stayed where she was for a minute. Not for anything was she moving upstairs. But however hard her bed on the floor should prove, she was so deadly deadly tired she knew she'd have no trouble at all in getting to sleep.

CHAPTER TWO

DALE was sure of nothing when she woke to another day. She'd been dreaming of Andrew, crying in her sleep—the usual thing since their break-up. Yet the minute she opened her tear-wet eyes she was bang slap in the present, with something completely unexpected to be dealt with. She had to reconcile herself to the fact that Beth, her mother-figure, was gone for ever, and gone for ever too the world of childhood and picnics and governesses, to which she'd sought to return. She had to reconcile herself to the fact that she was here at Jackalass where she had wanted to be, but instead of being in the midst of a comfortable family, she was alone with the unpredictable Trelawney Saber.

She scrambled off her mattress on the floor, which hadn't really been very comfortable. She'd better shower, dress, start something moving—get his breakfast. Not that he was incapacitated, but he might not be feeling very bri this morning; he was sure to have a hangover. She l at herself in the glass and with a grimace reached like brush. That hair-cut! She was like a scarecrow, thought was just as well since she was cooped up wi Trelawney Saber. She brightened a little though he'd that Rebie would be back today—he'd sai added a laconic, 'Maybe'. But why? Wouldn't Rebie come back to make sure he was all right? The wonder was that she hadn't come back with him yesterday, when it had happened. Someone should have come. But of course he was one of those men who like to be independent—tough. His image flitted through her mind—the way he'd looked last night pouring whisky into the tea mugs, his striped shirt hanging outside his pants, his feet bare, that—cynical look on his lean suntanned face. Yes, he *was* tough. Full stop.

When she went to the kitchen—showered, dressed in black jeans and sleeveless vest—it was hot already, sizzlingly hot, and he was already up and about. He'd even breakfasted; Dale could smell steak and coffee. But he drifted into the kitchen while she was sitting on a stool at the kitchen table, buttering some biscuits to eat with the tea she'd made.

'Getting everything you want?'

His voice made her start, and she turned quickly, almost knocking over her cup. There he stood, looking across at her quizzically, wearing shoes this morning, tan and polished, and clean buff pants with a dark red shirt. His face wasn't as drawn as it had been last night, but he was unsmiling, and she had the instant feeling he thought her nuisance, and would sooner she wasn't around to bother . Well, she wasn't going to bother him. She was going p well out of his way. There were plenty of things ld find to do before Rebie came, which she hoped head his morning. She might even make some bread.

He said fine,' she told him. 'You needn't worry your cuits, Dale ging, and after finishing buttering her biscuits, meditatively. over at him again. He was staring at her

'Little Daisy Driscoll!' he said musingly. 'Looking just as if you've spent the last ten years asleep in the middle of the mulga. Not in the least grown up.' His gaze moved down her figure then back to her face. 'I hope the black garb doesn't have any significance. Your father——?'

'My father's alive and well, thank you.' She said it touchily because his attitude disconcerted her, as did the expression on his face. 'I just happen to like black, that's all.'

'Pity,' he said briefly. 'It doesn't do a thing for you, you know. Personally, I find it depressing.'

A tremor ran along her nerves. 'Do you really?' she said coolly. 'That doesn't bother me particularly, I'm afraid. And you don't have to stand there staring at me all day, you know. You can—you can take your hangover somewhere else!' She turned her head away and began rather angrily to eat her biscuits.

Two minutes passed before he said imperturbably, 'I was right last night, wasn't I? This *is* another disaster period. Do you need some help? Why don't you come out with it, Daisy? I can be very sympathetic if it's required.' He came across the room to sit on the edge of the table and look down at her. 'What's gone sour on you, chicken?'

Chicken! Indignation surged over her in a flood. He talked to her as though she were a child—and that was how he saw her. Asleep in the mulga for the last ten years! If he only knew the anguish she'd been through—was still going through. 'Don't patronise me,' she wanted to tell him. 'I was in love—it's all ended—he's found someone else, and it's been agony.'

She lifted her head and on the point of telling him, she met his eyes. Her parted lips closed without her having uttered a word. She couldn't possibly tell him. He'd probably snap his fingers—laugh, talk about calf love, especially if he knew she hadn't even slept with Andrew. He wouldn't understand love the way she'd experienced it. He was the kind of man who took love lightly, wherever he found it. 'Come on now, chicken,' she could imagine him saying. 'You'll get over it, you haven't exactly been seduced and betrayed, have you?'

'Nothing's gone sour on me,' she said after a moment. 'There's not a thing to tell.'

'Liar,' he said lightly. 'You'd have talked to Beth about it. That's what you wanted when you came here, isn't it? But you won't talk to me.' He got to his feet. 'Okay, darling. But if you change your mind don't underestimate my willingness to comfort a female who needs comforting.'

'I don't need comforting, thank you,' was all Dale said, though she was quivering. What exactly did he mean by comforting?

He walked nonchalantly from the room, and she drew a deep breath of relief. She didn't know where he was off to; possibly the office. The outstation affairs were his business, seeing the run now belonged to him.

She finished her meal, and decided to tidy up in readiness for Rebie, because she and Rebie would have a whole lot to catch up on, a load of memories to share. They wouldn't want to be wasting time on housework. Perhaps she'd be able to talk to Rebie about Andrew, though she wasn't altogether sure of that. It all depended how they got on together. Ten years was a long time.

She washed the breakfast dishes, including Trelawney's, then went out to Mrs Miller's room to dismantle her bed and pack up her personal belongings. She carted everything back upstairs, and was thankful Trelawney wasn't a witness, because it was awkward getting the mattress up the stairs, and he couldn't have helped, in his condition. She made his bed, and got out of his room as fast as she could, to

look into the other bedrooms and decide which one was
Rebie's. She discovered luggage in two of the rooms, be-
longing, presumably, to the guests—the Richards. One
male, one female, she assessed, from one or two things lying
about. Rebie's room was obviously the one with the twin
beds in it. Lots of clothes in the half-open wardrobe, litter
all over the dressing table, shoes scattered across the floor.
She'd been untidy as a child and clearly was so now.

Dale made up one of the beds for herself and reminisced
about Rebie as she did so. She'd been a harmlessly naughty
child, and she had manipulated people while Dale stood by
and watched and marvelled. If she wanted chocolates from
the store, she told her father her mother had said she might
have some. If her mother queried it—Dad had given her
the sweets as a reward, or they were for Daisy, because
she was a long way from home. And she'd been the ring-
leader in games of teasing the governess. How often they'd
hidden when it was time to start lessons—and how often
Rebie had pretended to be stupid so that Arnoldine had
to explain the one thing to her over and over again until
she was almost out of her mind, and the whole lesson was
wasted. Then Rebie would put on a great act of suddenly
understanding it all, while Dale and young David and
little Joanna tried to suppress their giggles.

Dale was smiling a little as she turned her attention to
her suitcase, to see what needed to be hung up and what
could stay folded away. It didn't look as if anything needed
to be hung up, she decided after no more than a few
seconds' perusal of the very limited gear she'd brought. In
her depressed and overwrought state, she'd chosen the
oldest and most unattractive clothes she owned—things
dating from three or four years before, when she'd thought
that to wear black—very casual black at that—was adult
and 'with it'. Into her bag had gone the old black jeans, the

black cotton vests and sagging T-shirts, and a skivvy with a low scooped neckline. Apart from that, there were two pairs of blue denim shorts, pyjamas, a bikini, black sandals and a pair of black and white jogging shoes. She must have been mad, she thought now, somewhat appalled. Not a dress—not a single dress she could wear for dinner, if everyone were dressing up a little. The thing was, she'd felt all her pretty clothes had been for Andrew, and since she'd lost him, what did it matter how she looked? She didn't want to attract men—quite the contrary, in fact. Anyhow, if necessary, Rebie would lend her something, provided their heights and figures weren't too dissimilar.

She closed the lid down on her suitcase of decidedly depressing clothes and went downstairs.

Through the big fly-screen windows she could see Trelawney lounging in a deck chair in the shade of the mango trees, reading a thinnish book that probably had something to do with cattle raising. He glanced up as Dale emerged from the house, and asked her, 'Where are you off to?'

'Just to look around.'

'You'll need a hat,' he said, and returned to his reading.

Dale pulled a face. He was right, of course. But she hadn't brought a hat with her—another bit of stupidity. She hadn't even brought the sunblock cream she'd always used in Rockhampton. Standing in the tree shade she looked across the garden into blinding sunlight, felt herself screwing up her eyes, felt lines begin to form there already. She didn't even have any sunglasses, and though she'd been squinting into the sun when she'd been driving, she hadn't cared. Now she thought of the store; there'd be hats there. But she didn't want to ask Trelawney to unlock the store for her. She had no right to, anyhow, she was an uninvited guest here, after all. Maybe she should just go inside and look for a hat in one of the cupboards.

Though what did it really matter if she did get the skin burnt off her nose? Who cared?

Trelawney was ignoring her now, and she felt infuriated. Was he annoyed with her for not taking up his invitation to—to tell him all? She certainly didn't want *him* to comfort her. A shiver ran through her. Exactly what had he meant by saying he was willing to comfort her? Not—*that*, she assured herself. Not with his chest strapped up and probably painful. Besides, she couldn't fool herself he found her attractive. She simply wasn't . . .

She went inside and found a hat—a straw hat with a wide but battered brim. It would have to do, and after all it was only good sense to protect her face. Trelawney looked up when she came out again, and plainly he wasn't impressed, though he made no comment. He just studied her as though she were some weird object that he couldn't quite fathom—What is it? Beast or bird or fish? Dale hated being looked at that way, but she wasn't going to let him know it.

'Before I go,' she said, standing motionless and in full view so he could squint at her all he liked, 'when do you expect Rebie will arrive?'

'I wouldn't even try to guess,' he said unhelpfully, and returned to his book.

Dale marched off.

She spent what was left of the morning in the garden and down by the lagoon. By the woodheap she encountered the cowboy, and to her pleasure it was Fred, who had been here in her day—his stiff leg a little stiffer, his face a little more leathery, still laconic, still with nothing much to say other than a cheery, 'G'day!' Though as she stood watching him chopping wood, he stopped work suddenly to give her a piercing look from his bright blue eyes and exclaim, 'Cer-rripes! It's Daisy!'

Dale nodded, pleased.

'Where you been all this time, Daisy?' He wiped the perspiration from around his neck with a large dark handkerchief, which he then stuffed back into his pants pocket.

'Oh—in Gladstone with my father and stepmother and the children,' she said, glossing over everything that had happened. 'How's everything been going here?'

'Quietened down,' he said. 'Cook went over to Warathar after the boss and the missus left here. Stayed there when Trelawney took over. No one around now the muster's on ... You looking after Trelawney, are you? Saw him come in yesterday—put some food in the fridge.'

'Yes, I'm looking after him,' Dale agreed. After all, she had washed his dishes and made his bed, and she was perfectly prepared to make him some lunch. She didn't elaborate or mention the accident, and Fred nodded, and began to chop again. Conversation over.

Dale watched him for a while, and then she looked back towards the garden, half hidden behind a tangle of red bougainvillaea. Traveller's palms traced their beautiful fan shapes against the blue of the sky, and her nostrils caught the subtle perfume of the red oleander flowers that grew in a thick hedge along by the vegetable garden. These were things she remembered from her childhood, part of the background of life here. They were the same now as they had been then except that she was probably more consciously aware of them now that she was older, and oddly, they made her realise how much she had changed since last she was here. She was a different person entirely. And all the people she had known when she had lived here—they must be different too. She began to walk slowly on towards the lagoon, and her thoughts moved to Trelawney Saber. He'd changed too—he must have, and not just physically. She'd been so very young ten years ago, she knew little more about him except that he was fun on a picnic, and that his love affairs got him into trouble. For all she knew, he might have settled down, his wild oats sown.

And Arnoldine, the pretty governess, her thoughts ran on. She'd be in her late thirties now. Was she still pretty? Was she still in love with Trelawney—after all this time? After all, she wasn't married.

It was funny, but when Dale had packed up and left Rockhampton for the sanctuary of Jackalass, it hadn't occurred to her how different it would all be. The place was the same—the lagoon, the yellow grass, the homestead among its trees—but it was the people she had tried to come back to. Motherly Aunt Beth, the children in a children's world. That was all gone. Now she could only hope there would still be a strong link between herself and Rebie.

The day passed and Rebie didn't come. Dale made lunch for herself and Trelawney, and then she made some bread. She spent most of the afternoon in the hot kitchen, while Trelawney simply kept out of her way. As she prepared dinner, she wondered what he'd have done if she hadn't been here.

When she'd taken the steak and salad into the living room and they were sitting at the table, she remarked nervously, 'I thought Rebie would be here by now.'

He made no comment, and Dale looked at her meal without appetite. She began to wish she'd left her mattress in Mrs Miller's room; she didn't fancy sleeping upstairs. Yet where was the difference? she argued with herself. A man with broken ribs wasn't likely to jump on anyone. She glanced at Trelawney covertly, and saw that he was enjoying his dinner and looking very much at his ease. And he wasn't making any attempt at conversation; he evidently didn't think her worth the trouble, she thought resentfully.

It wasn't until he'd finished eating that he remarked, 'You know how to cook a steak, Daisy. Aren't you enjoying it?'

'I'm not hungry. I'm worried about Rebie.'

'Then for heaven's sake quit worrying about her. She's all right. If she comes she comes, if she doesn't there's nothing you or I can do about it. If you don't think to warn people you're about to visit them, you know, you just have to take pot luck when it comes to who's going to be around. I'm benefiting from your presence, at any rate,' he concluded with a crooked smile.

'Are you? I don't get the feeling you're particularly pleased to have me around,' she said perversely.

'Oh, come on—you've cooked me an excellent meal, and I've appreciated it. If you're feeling neglected, it's because I haven't felt much like talking today.'

'All that whisky you drank last night,' she put in swiftly, and his eyebrows rose.

'If that's how you choose to read it. However, I was about to thank you for tidying my bed—for feeding me. Ordinarily I'd cope with those things myself.'

'I thought Arnoldine was looking after you.'

'At Warathar—sure,' he said smoothly. 'But I'm talking about the present situation. Admittedly, I'm not feeling a hundred per cent, but left to myself I'd still have eaten something . . . You know, Daisy, you should learn to accept a compliment more gracefully. It's a good thing in a woman.' His gaze moved to her hair as he spoke, and she interpreted the half smile on his face as a recognition of the fact that few compliments would come the way of a girl who looked like she did. If he only knew—Andrew used to shower her with compliments, and if she wanted to, she could look quite stunning. Well, not now, she thought uneasily, not with this haircut.

She stood up and reached for his plate. 'Do you want tea or coffee?'

'Coffee. And I prefer it filtered, not percolated. We'll have it in the garden—we might as well enjoy the night air.'

Dale listened without comment. She supposed she would do as he said. She didn't want to put in the evening alone, but she couldn't hide from herself the fact that she didn't feel at ease with Trelawney Saber. There was too much of the unknown about him, and if he hadn't been in the mood for talking today then neither was she in the mood for exerting herself to cope with a strange male, at this exact period of her life.

She found filter papers and made the coffee the way he liked, and as she fixed the tray she reflected that it was supposed to help mend a broken heart to get out and meet new people, do new things. She wasn't too sure of that. She'd planned to tell Aunt Beth the sad story of her life, but now she had to bottle it all up. So which was the better treatment? To get it off your chest, or to talk about something else and hope it would all go away?

With Trelawney, she had no choice. She *had* to pretend nothing was wrong. She wasn't in the least tempted to make a confession to him and ask him for—comfort . . .

'Now let's hear what's been happening to you since you left Jackalass all those years ago,' he said some minutes later, as they sat in the old deck chairs in the flower-scented garden, drinking their coffee. The air was velvet-soft and warm, a few crickets were chirping, and Dale could hear the tiny flying foxes squeaking away up in the mango trees.

'Nothing exciting's been happening,' she said.

He made a wry face. 'I'm hardly expecting an adventure story. But as I remember, your father had married again, and when you turned up here you were like a motherless calf—all big eyes and desperation.'

'I suppose so,' she conceded. 'I thought I was never going to see my father again. He'd wanted to send me to boarding school for a term, but Olivia said the summer holidays were too close and too long, and she wouldn't be ready for me. I just couldn't understand, but I suppose she was rather young—only twenty-three—and she just didn't want a nine- or ten-year-old kid around as soon as she came back from her honeymoon. Actually it was her mother who had the idea of sending me away to a family in the country. Uncle David is some kind of distant relative of hers, you see.'

Dale paused. She remembered it all so clearly. Mrs Walters, Olivia's mother, telling her father, 'Dale's such a peaky little thing. A spell in the country would do wonders for her. There are other children there—it's a big family. They do correspondence lessons with a governess. She'd love it. Isn't it just the ideal solution?'

Dale had had no say in it at all. Snap! It was all decided. No one thought to ask her if she'd like to go to the country, no one thought to give her any kind of an idea as to what she might expect. In no time at all she was whizzed off to Townsville and put on a plane by Mrs Walters.

'I had no idea how long I was being sent away for,' she said aloud. 'I thought it might be for ever.'

'It was over two years, wasn't it? How did that happen?'

'Mostly because of Olivia's health. She had a miscarriage —I heard about that years later—and when she was pregnant again she had to be careful. Then—well, Stuart was a delicate baby, he needed all her attention. I've sort of pieced it all together since—all the things they never explained——'

'So how was it when you went back?' His voice in the darkness sounded sympathetic, interested enough.

'Not really good,' Dale said flatly. 'Stuart was still a baby—about sixteen months old—and Kimmie was due at any moment. That's why I had to stay here till the holidays were almost over—you left just before I did, as a matter of fact. I went practically straight to boarding school. If they'd let me go to the same school as Rebie it would have helped, but it had all been arranged. I went home for holidays, of course, but I'd sooner have come here. Aunt Beth used to write, but not often. I think she played it down so as to leave the field clear for my own family to take over.'

'And did they take over?'

'I suppose so. But I guess it's always at least a little hard for an older child with small stepbrothers and sisters. I was useful to help with the little ones, of course, and Olivia could hardly be expected to love me the way she loved her own children. I accept that now, though I couldn't see it that way at the time, and I suspect my father was—restrained, because he didn't want her to be jealous. She was, though. I could feel it.'

He didn't press her for details, which she wouldn't have given in any case, but asked, 'What career did you take up, Daisy? Or were you a fixture in the home—a Cinderella?'

'No, nothing like that,' she said quickly, wondering if he thought she *looked* like a Cinderella. 'I didn't take up a career, really. I worked in a furniture and decorating shop —making soft furnishings mostly, though I was learning something about colour schemes and fabrics and so on.'

'You enjoyed that?'

'Yes,' she said shortly, and there was a long pause.

'Well then, what are the missing pieces? Why did you go bush? Or are you just taking time off?'

Dale had an inward struggle with herself. It wouldn't be true to say she was taking time off, but she had no intention of providing Trelawney with what he called the missing pieces.

'I'm not sure. I just thought I'd like to get away,' she said finally.

'From what? Not from your job, I take it. So—from whom? Your stepmother? The kids?'

'No, they've all moved to Brisbane,' she said nervily. 'I wanted to see everyone here, that's all.'

'Is it?' he said sceptically. 'Oh well, keep it all to yourself if that's the way you want it. I'm not particular. It just occurred to me that talking it out can be therapeutic.'

'There's nothing to talk out,' said Dale. 'I told you that before.'

'Nevertheless, you have the air of a minor tragedy queen,' he drawled. 'Unshed tears in your eyes, no appetite, pallor—touchiness.'

'I'm run down,' she said quickly.

'Working too hard? Okay, I'll mind my own business.'

Silence.

Dale broke it by asking awkwardly, 'Where did you go when you left here?'

'I took a job on a cattle station in the Territory. I stayed there four or five years, then I went to Spain—South America—and came back to help the old man on the stud farm.'

'And he left it to Ray, not to you.'

'Sure, that pleased us both. Ray and Stephanie always had an eye on the Darling Downs. My affinity is with Warathar and the Gulf country—battling with the Wet, struggling to know the unknowable—this is where I want to be. It's my—heavenly home. Is that understandable to you? Do you like the Gulf?'

'I don't *really* know much about it,' she said slowly. 'I was a child when I lived here, I didn't really know what it was all about. I was happy here, though—safe. Part of a family. I liked the people, and my lessons—and the picnics! I'll never forget swimming out at the waterhole. It was beautiful. There's been nothing like that since.'

'We'll go there tomorrow,' he said.

She stared at him. 'What about Rebie?'

'If Rebie turns up, she'll still be around when we come back. We'll take your car and you can drive. I'm treating myself with care for a few days. And in fact right now I'm going to take myself inside and go upstairs to bed. Are you coming?'

'Not—yet,' she said, vaguely embarrassed.

Trelawney stood up and looked down at her through the darkness.

'You're not sleeping on the floor again tonight, I hope.'

'No. I—I made up a bed in Rebie's room.'

'Good. You'll be more comfortable there. Sweet dreams, then. I'm going to have a nip of whisky. Will you join me?'

'No, thank you,' she said stiffly.

A minute later, through one of the big wire gauzed windows, she could see him in the living room—pouring his drink, tipping his head back and swallowing it down. She watched him intently, as if she expected to learn something about him. She knew so little, and how much of it had been magnified by the eyes of a child she had no idea. All the same, she was sure he was a man in whose life sex played an important part. He was so—whole and so masculine.

Presently he crossed the room and went upstairs, and

light fell from the verandah into the garden. Dale stayed where she was, waiting. Waiting for what? For him to get to bed and fall asleep? She could hardly sit here half the night just to be sure he was unconscious before she too went up the stairs. Asleep or awake, he was not interested in her. Quite plainly, he regarded her more or less as the child she'd still been when last they'd met. Why, tomorrow he was giving her a treat—taking her out to the waterhole. Dale hoped Rebie would arrive in time to come with them. Her eyes narrowed a little as she thought about Rebie. Why hadn't she come back today? Didn't she care that Trelawney was alone and injured? Of course he was capable of looking after himself, but wouldn't any girl— any woman—want to help him? Dale simply couldn't fathom it.

She remained wrapped in her thoughts for some time, and it wasn't until she found she had started to fall asleep in her chair that she forced herself to her feet and went inside. For the first time she began to wonder if she should have acted so hastily—left her job, left Rockhampton, cut herself off. All her clothes and other belongings were packed away in boxes and suitcases ready to move to wherever she went to next. She'd told Sally where she was going, and suggested she should find a new flatmate. Sally knew her love affair with Andrew was over, but she didn't know how much it had hurt, how shattered she was. Now Dale asked herself if she shouldn't have stayed, put up a fight. Perhaps she'd have won Andrew back, because they'd been very much in love.

Though perhaps it was only she who had been so much in love. Maybe Andrew had never seen it as a lasting thing. All he'd wanted might have been an affair—and to get her into bed with him. And because she hadn't let it happen—finis. And after all, she reminded herself as she rather slowly climbed the stairs, you can't put up a fight for someone who is ignoring you.

The hurt of it all came back achingly, and she swallowed down a sob. All that had been hers he had given to another girl. How could he? Oh, how could he? And that other girl—would he ask her to marry him? Oh God, was there nothing—*nothing* you could do to take away the pain when love is over? Sally had said carelessly. 'You'll forget him in no time, honey. I always make a list of the guy's faults when we come to the parting of the ways. You take a long hard look at Andrew and you'll be surprised what you can see in retrospect. Look—he never let you choose which movie you wanted to see, did he? Or which restaurant you'd like to dine at. Think of that!'

Dale had smiled palely, too proud to let Sally know how deep the hurt had gone, how much she wanted him back. Now, thinking about it all, she said half aloud, 'It didn't matter that I wasn't asked to choose—all I wanted was just to be with him, to go where he went.'

She was standing motionless on the verandah, staring into space. A strip of soft light came through the open door of Trelawney's room at the far end, and suddenly she was aware of it, and of the fact that he couldn't have gone to sleep yet. She was aware too that her face was wet with tears, and she pulled a tissue from the pocket of her jeans and blew her nose.

'Daisy!'

Her heart jumped and she glanced fearfully along the verandah. But Trelawney didn't appear. He must want something, she though agitatedly. Water—aspirin—another pillow. She dabbed desperately at her eyes and her cheeks.

'What?' she called out huskily.

'What the hell are you bawling about?'

Taken aback, she swallowed hard.

'I'm not bawling. I was just blowing my nose.'

'You were bawling, I heard you. Come and tell me all about it—come on.' He sounded weary, impatient.

'I'm on my way to bed,' she said petulantly. 'I'm tired.'

'You won't sleep. You'd better get it off your chest. Things never seem so bad when you've talked about them. Come on, come on, I won't eat you.'

Dale said nothing for a long moment. The awful thing was, she was tempted, she who had been so certain earlier that she *wasn't* tempted. There was something in Trelawney's voice that made her feel weak, confessional, as if she could go and sit on the side of his bed and pour it all out, just the way she would have done to Beth. Pour it all out and have a good long cry. So far, she hadn't allowed herself that kind of relief. Sharing a room with Sally had been restrictive, and driving here, along the hundreds of miles of outback roads—true enough there had often been tears on her cheeks, tears that had soon dried up in the heat, but they hadn't been exactly therapeutic. And the two nights she'd stayed in hotels, she'd been too dead tired to lie awake crying. So she could really do with a cry. But—on Trelawney Saber's shoulder? With Trelawney Saber's arms about her—even if he saw her merely as an unattractive and immature little female creature? Definitely not. That would be asking for trouble!

'No,' she said, and added shakily, 'Thank you.'

'Then for pity's sake, shut up,' he snapped back. 'I don't enjoy the prospect of lying here listening to you howling half the night.'

Dale didn't answer. She went into Rebie's room and slammed the door.

CHAPTER THREE

SHE got up early next day—earlier than Trelawney—and cooked breakfast for the two of them. She told him she'd slept well, and asked after his ribs, and decided that after all it was easy enough to come to terms with the situation. It was awkward, but only if you saw it that way. After all, nothing had happened in the night. She had slept in her room and Trelawney had slept in his. He couldn't insist she should tell him about herself, and she could keep the sad story of her love affair to herself.

This morning some of the lines had disappeared from his face. His hair was smoothly combed and still wet from the shower, and Dale could smell the after-shave cologne he used. He didn't seem nearly so intimidatingly hard-bitten.

'How's your mood today?' he asked into her thoughts. 'Still ready to take that expedition to the waterhole?'

'Yes, I'd like that,' she agreed. 'But if you're not feeling up to it, I can find the way there on my own.'

'For God's sake, why wouldn't I be feeling up to it?' he said irritably. 'It's hardly a marathon event. What do you want to do? Pack up a picnic and make a day of it?'

Dale had already thought about that. 'I want to wash out some clothes this morning. And if we don't leave too early, Rebie might be here. This afternoon will do.'

'Well, we can't stay in all day waiting for Rebie. What's wrong, anyhow? Is the idea of going out alone with me making you jittery? I'm incapacitated, harmless—well, almost,' he added dryly.

She looked across the table and met his eyes. His appraisal of her was cool and impersonal, and she didn't wonder. What she'd seen in the mirror this morning hadn't been very inspiring—the black clothes again and black smudges under her eyes to match. She had thought of rummaging in Rebie's drawers for something more cheerful to wear, and then discarded the idea. It didn't suit her mood to make herself look attractive. But curiously, it somehow hurt her pride to know that Trelawney found her unattractive. She *could* look nice, and it was hard to be plain.

She washed out some of her things after she'd done the breakfast dishes, and as well, she washed a couple of Trelawney's shirts. They were quality garments, and the red one had looked good on him despite the rib belt underneath. She hung them on the line carefully and went inside.

Still Rebie didn't come, but by now she had begun to take it philosophically. Rebie must know he was self-sufficient, and she probably had to stay at the muster camp with the guests. If Trelawney wanted, there was nothing in this world to stop him getting through to Warathar on the telephone and having someone drive over here for him. He didn't have to stay at Jackalass, fending for himself and waiting for Rebie. And if he didn't want to leave Dale on her own, couldn't he invite her to Warathar? In which case, what would she do?

'I wouldn't go,' she decided. She'd come here to see the Vinings, and see them she would.

At lunch she asked Trelawney how long it would be before the muster was over.

'A week—two weeks,' he told her carelessly. 'Is it too long for you to wait?'

'No. I told you I've left my job. But Kevin might not like me staying here.'

'Now don't talk nonsense! We're hospitable people in the Gulf country. Can you see Kevin turning you out? He'll be tickled pink you've come. The pity is that the family's broken up. It's a disappointment for you, isn't it?'

She nodded. That was something she couldn't deny.

'You're lucky I'm here,' he remarked, getting up from the table. 'You could have come to a completely empty house. As it is you've got me to keep you company and tell you what's been happening.'

'I'd have found out from Fred,' said Dale, getting up from the table too and beginning to clear the dishes.

'And then what would you have done?' he asked mockingly.

'I don't know. I might have gone out to the muster camp.'

'Is that what you want to do?'

'I—not if Rebie's coming back. I might as well wait. If you're sure she is coming——'

'Oh, she'll be back. She and the others from the big smoke will have had enough of it before the muster's over ... Anyway, why don't you run off and get your swimming things if you want to go to the waterhole. Leave the dishes.'

Dale ran off.

'Maybe I should go out to the muster camp,' she thought as she rummaged through her suitcase in the bedroom, found her bikini and a towel. She couldn't fool herself her presence was essential to Trelawney, and yet she didn't really want to go to the muster. She wasn't ready to cope with a world that lacked privacy and comfort too. She remembered that she and Rebie and young David and Joanna had on a couple of occasions spent a night at the muster camp. Despite the dust and the heat and the flies, she still retained an impression of excitement—of the ringers riding in, of the crack of stockwhips, of the bellowing of the cattle as they trampled round in the dust, tossing their horns. It might be fine to go there now if she could take part, but she'd be absolutely useless. She hadn't ridden a horse since she left Jackalass.

So—she was staying here.

She put on the bikini under her jeans and vest and wished that she had a one-piece swimsuit. She'd lost weight since Andrew ditched her, and looking at herself critically in the glass before she pulled on her vest, she knew she was far from at her best. Oh well, she didn't want to be admired, so what the heck? She settled for black jeans in preference to the blue denim shorts too, and if Trelawney found her clothes depressing, she couldn't be worried.

Not much later, they were on their way to the waterhole. Dale had expected to be driving, but he'd changed his mind about that. Broken ribs or not, he was taking the wheel.

'At least I know what to expect this way,' he told her unflatteringly. 'I'm more practised at dodging potholes than you are too, that's certain.'

The air was hot and humid, and Dale sat beside him in the front seat. The windows were open, and, eyes narrowed against the sun, she stared out, musing, trying to remember driving this way before and not succeeding terribly well.

'Remember?' Trelawney asked once, and she said vaguely. 'Oh, more or less. But we used to talk and sing all the way when Arnie drove us to the waterhole. We took the scenery for granted.'

She couldn't do that now. The singing, stinging colours were so beautiful. Red earth, purple shadows, yellow-flowered bushes. (They'd called them ant bushes, she re-

membered, because they were always alive with ants.)
White cockatoos flew up from the grass and she gave a little
gasp of pleasure. Though the birds were among her strong-
est memories, she'd never got such a kick out of them as
she did now. It was as if she had long ago tasted something
ambrosial, and now, with a palate that was no longer innocent, had come back to discover the full magical
flavour...

The creek took a big turn between the homestead and the
waterhole, and for that reason they didn't stick to it, but
followed a track that was barely discernible—through the
endless tufts of Mitchell grass that at this time of year
looked dry as straw, but from which, after even an inch
of rain, green shoots would come with miraculous speed.
It didn't look, from the overgrown state of the track, as if
many trips were made to the waterhole these days—another sign of how things had changed.

'Are you going to swim?' she asked Trelawney.

'No. You can have the water to yourself. I'm going to
relax.'

'Perhaps you shouldn't be doing this,' she remarked
anxiously. 'Why don't you let me drive? I'll be really careful.' The car hit a bump as she spoke and she lurched
against him.

'For heaven's sake!' he exclaimed irritably. 'We're nearly
there. Just shut up and let me concentrate.'

'I'm—concerned for your welfare,' she said, hurt.

'Then don't be. It's pointless. I can make my own decisions, and I don't have a predilection for mother-hen
types. Your little chirrupings are tiresome.'

Dale bit her lip angrily and said no more. She was concerned for him—any girl would be. But he seemed intent
on rejecting even normal consideration. She had hardly
been behaving like a mother hen. No wonder Rebie hadn't

hurried back to Jackalass, she thought.

The pool was as she remembered it, but even more beautiful. She completely forgot Trelawney Saber as she stripped off vest and jeans, discarded her sandals, and walked down the sandy bank to kneel down in the shade and peer into the pool as she had when she was a child. Clear water, the green water-fern—the nardoo—like something imprisoned in glass. Pebbles shining bright and smooth, the reflections of the white gums and pandanus palms that stood on the banks. She'd seen ibises wading here, seen pelicans sailing, grotesque yet enchanting, seen the trees full of green chattering budgerigars and tiny finches.

After a long time she slid into the water, gently and slowly, as if to disturb it as little as possible. She floated on her back, and it was heavenly. On the coast she had swum in the sea, but this was different. The water was so soft and limpid and secluded with the trees hanging over. For a long time more she floated and swam and waded and stared, remembering her childhood, feeling the ache of nostalgia. Children's voices, the building of dams, the games of make-believe, the joy of the water after the heat of the sun. It had all been so good, so uncomplicated. There'd been no hurt such as Andrew had inflicted on her Children's squabbles and children's tears. It could never be like that again. The nearest thing would be to have children of one's own—watch them grow up here, play the same games, have the same enjoyments. She'd dreamed of having Andrew's children till not very long ago——

She looked up and saw that Trelawney, who had gone for a walk along the bank, was now sitting on a great flat boulder. She was grateful for his silence and for the fact that he was ignoring her, and not interrupting her rather sombre musings. Then as she waded through the shallows and suddenly found herself only a few feet away from the man on the bank, she came back to a sharp awareness of the present. He was looking at her hard, his blue-green eyes intent and critical, and she was instantly conscious of how little of her the bikini concealed.

She left the water hurriedly, her one thought being to get to her towel, dry off, pull on her clothes. A spell had been broken, the real world had surged back—and it wasn't the world of children. Not with Trelawney Saber looking at her like that. She was burningly aware of the unattractiveness of her figure since she'd lost weight. When she'd gone swimming with Andrew, he'd never looked at her so dispassionately, so assessingly. She'd always had a flat stomach, a firm diaphragm, good legs, but now the prominence of her collarbone, the boniness of her hips, the fact that her rib cage showed—all these things made her sure she must look a sight. Top that with short wet hair, sticking out all over the place, and it was easy to imagine the impression she made on the man who was studying her so openly.

She stood stock still as he addressed her.

'You know, Daisy, you're not at all the kid I've been thinking you. Twenty-one ... Stripped, you look older. Nothing of the child left about you.'

Dale rarely blushed, but she did so now, hotly and uncomfortably.

'I've lost weight lately,' she managed, simply because she had to say something.

'I guessed that. What's been going on inside your head while you've been mooning about in the water? You've been thinking some long thoughts, haven't you?'

'Not—really,' she stammered. 'I was just remembering when I was here before, that's all.'

'I imagine so. But what else?' he asked dryly. 'Come on,

sit down here and tell me. And if you say once again in that martyred way that there's nothing to tell, then so help me I'll shake it out of you!'

He paused and Dale heard herself swallow nervously. Then he reached out for her wrist, twisting her arm and pulling her down forcibly so she was compelled to sit on the boulder beside him. Helpless, she winced, and promised herself she wouldn't talk to him—wouldn't tell him one single thing about Andrew.

Angrily, through clenched teeth, she said, 'You shouldn't exert yourself like that. You'll hurt your chest.'

'I've hurt my chest,' he agreed, keeping hold of her wrist. 'If I shake you, I'll hurt it more. But don't imagine that's going to stop me ... Start talking.'

'I—can't,' she said helplessly, averting her face.

'Can't? What claptrap! Nothing's so bad you can't talk about it,' he retorted cruelly. 'It's a man, isn't it? What happened?'

His fingers were biting into her flesh, and despite the heat she shivered. She blurted out resentfully, 'If you must know, I—he—he dropped me.'

'Yes, go on—spill it out—let's hear the rest. Come on, confession is good for the soul—you'll feel a new woman once you've got it all out.'

Dale's tongue came out to moisten her soft upper lip. She saw a lizard dart across the rock, pause, then slither on. She didn't want to tell Trelawney a thing, but he was utterly intent on making her talk. She thought painfully of Andrew, of the wonder of their love affair—of her happiness that had ended so abruptly. And she knew she couldn't expose it to his cynicism. Her head lowered, she asked him, 'Isn't that enough? He dropped me. We—we were in love and now it's all over.'

'Love affairs have begun and ended before this,' he said

realistically. 'It's happening every day. Haven't you been through it before?'

She shook her head. 'I—I never loved anyone else.'

She felt his eyes probing her face, and sensed he was beginning to take her more seriously. 'You mean you loved him? You weren't just—in love?'

'Of course I—of course——' She swallowed, unable to go on. She could feel his fingers warm against her flesh, caressing now, rather than cruel, and with a violent movement she pulled her arm away from him. 'Of course I loved him. Terribly—terribly.' Her voice broke. 'Is that what you want to know?'

'It's not a matter of what I want to know. It's a matter of the necessity for you to put it into words,' he said with a calm that hurt. He leaned forward a little, his hands between his knees, and the sun shone through the trees on the tawny colour of his hair, brightening it. 'Have you talked to anyone else—or were you counting on Beth?'

'I haven't talked,' she said. 'And I don't want to now. Not to you. Stop—stop fussing over me like a mother hen,' she added with a flash of spirit. 'You're not the only one who can make your own decisions. I can make mine too— on my own.' Her mouth trembled and she wanted to cry. She shouldn't have told him a thing. She'd known perfectly well he wouldn't really be sympathetic. He seemed to think it was all so simple that talking could cure her—and it couldn't. 'Talking doesn't change a damned thing,' she said aloud, her voice shaking.

'Except possibly your own angle,' he suggested. 'I take it that feeling the way you did you went to bed with him——'

She lifted her head, but instead of denying it she said accusingly, 'I suppose you're going to be clever and tell me that it serves me right—that that's the way to lose a man, giving in to him before he's married you.' In her case, she reflected, the exact opposite seemed to have happened, so it was no use being wise.

'No, I wasn't going to tell you that, as a matter of fact,' he said. 'I'm not a moralist, and besides, it's a consequence that doesn't necessarily follow, particularly these days.'

She turned her head slightly and found herself looking straight into his eyes, and a shock went through her. His expression was so different from anything she'd expected; the mockery, the derision, weren't there. His eyes, intent, looked at her as—as an equal, and with an inward tremor she realised *why* he looked at her that way. He thought she'd slept with Andrew. She hadn't said so, but that was how he understood it. Her lips parted on a denial, and then after all she said nothing. She'd be demoted back to child status if he knew. He'd stop taking her seriously. And what business of his was it, after all?

'Just how final is the break?' he asked, his glance moving quickly down the slenderness of her body and back again.

'Oh, it's quite final,' she said. 'There's someone else.' She drew up her knees and wrapped her arms around them concealingly.

'I see. Then at the risk of being told not to be impertinent, I'm going to ask you something. Do you—er—have some special problem that you wanted to confide to Beth?'

'Some special problem?' she repeated, mystified. 'What do you mean?'

'For God's sake, do I have to spell it out?' His mouth twisted so that the scar in his cheek deepened. 'I mean, are you pregnant?'

'No, I'm not!' Shocked, she jumped to her feet and stood with her back to him, unaware now of the beautiful water that shimmered under the trees, of the birds that flew there, of the fact that the sun was going down and the air was full of the pure red-gold that belongs to the outback.

She didn't hear him move, but in a couple of seconds he was standing behind her, and his arms had imprisoned her so that her body was drawn back against his. She heard herself gasp—felt his hands move swiftly up over her rib cage to cover her breasts burningly, and then, she didn't know how it happened, but he'd spun her round against him, and his hands were on her buttocks, bare except for the scrap of bikini.

It was all so quick, so wholly unexpected that she was too stunned to react and simply stared blankly into his face, her eyes locked in his. Her heart was pounding. So had he held Arnoldine Bell in his arms among the orange trees. But Arnie had been fully dressed ... And when he lowered his head, and his lips, brushing her forehead, the tip of her nose, moved on to the curve of her breast above the tiny bikini bra, she uttered a soft exclamation of alarm. And in her mind she could hear the little cries that Arnie had uttered that night ten years ago.

At that moment, as she realised later, she didn't think of Andrew. She'd never been in his arms like this—so close, so nakedly close. She could feel her heart pounding, and she waited almost passively for Trelawney to raise his head, for his lips to come against her mouth. Then she thought of Andrew—as Trelawney kissed her. She thought of him achingly, hungrily, and that was why she kissed Trelawney back, clinging to him, her eyes closed, aware of his hands on her buttocks, of his body pressed against her own.

Then with a groan he released her slightly, and she heard him mutter, 'Oh God, these damned ribs—I wish to hell I hadn't cracked them——'

Dale's eyes flew open. Crazily, she too wished he hadn't injured himself—she hadn't wanted him to let her go, she'd been drowning in his kiss, mindlessly slipping back to Andrew and the past—even though Andrew had never touched her this way—so possessively, so intimately. She must be mad, she thought, her startled eyes lingering on his face for a moment before she tore herself away from him and tried to control her breathing.

How had it happened? Easily enough for him, she supposed. It was an old habit—kissing any available female. But he shouldn't have started anything like this with her, and she shouldn't have let it happen—not when they were more or less isolated in the house at Jackalass. It was too dangerous. And besides—she stepped away from him and put the back of her hand against her warm, bruised mouth —she didn't want Trelawney Saber's kisses—or the kisses of any man. This, she supposed, was the comfort he'd been offering earlier. Well, it wasn't the kind of comfort she needed, and she felt more than slightly sickened by her own behaviour.

She took her hand from her mouth and raised her eyes. One end of his sensual mouth was curved upwards in a wry smile, and she told him quiveringly, 'I don't think that's a—a very good idea. For you to——'

'I don't either,' he agreed, the irony of his smile deepening. 'And believe it or not, it wasn't a thing I meant to do. If you'd had your clothes on it probably wouldn't have happened.'

Dale's eyes widened. Was he actually blaming the incident on her—insinuating that she'd deliberately tempted him? When it was he who had insisted she must sit down near him—talk—— As for her clothes, it was only because she'd been swimming that she was wearing nothing but her bikini.

'If you remember,' she said stiffly, 'I was on my way to get dressed. It was you who stopped me——'

'Okay, okay, then you should have run,' he said. He
put his hands over his eyes and drew them down his
cheeks, and she thought he was looking haggard again.
Almost as haggard as he'd looked the night she arrived
and found him so drunkenly asleep. 'I've got to tell you
something, Daisy. This had better not happen again.'

He paused, and she said hotly, 'Are you *really* blaming
me? If I'd run, you'd have caught me. Wouldn't you? You
—you *meant* to kiss me——'

He spread his hands. 'To kiss you—yes. I did have
that in mind. But not—— Well, it helped, didn't it? As
a bit of therapy. Weren't you imagining I was the guy who
dropped you?'

'No!' she said vehemently, and then, because that made
it seem even worse, 'Yes,' she breathed, and turned away
confused.

'I thought so ... But listen to me, Daisy.' He put his
hand on her bare shoulder and she flinched but didn't
move away. 'There's something you should know—Rebie
and I have just got ourselves engaged.'

What? Dale thought she must be going mad. She simply
couldn't believe what he had said. Trelawney Saber engaged to Rebie! Plump little Rebie, with her round face
and owl eyes—like herself, *years* younger than Trelawney!
It didn't make sense whichever way she looked at it.
Though—*that* was why Rebie was mixed up in the redecorating at Warathar. But why hadn't he told her about
the engagement right at the start, when he was bringing her
up to date on the doings of the Vining family?

'Why didn't you tell me before?' she asked him, her voice
uneven.

'It hardly seemed relevant,' he said ambiguously. 'In any
case, it's barely happened yet. No ring, no official announcement, no wedding date. It's all brand new.'

Dale's forehead wrinkled. 'Then why didn't Rebie come back with you? Why isn't she here?'

'We're not one flesh yet,' he said dryly, meaning exactly what she didn't know. 'And we're still two individuals, with our own desires.'

'But if she——' Dale stopped. If she loves you, she'd been going to say, and of course Rebie must love him, to be engaged to him. It was such a new concept she couldn't deal with it. Suddenly the day was too long. She felt exhausted. It was the heat—the emotion—all that enervating time she'd spent in the water, she thought confusedly. She said, 'I think it was despicable of you to—do what you did. But I suppose you thought you were quite safe, away out here with no one to see. Well, I'm not staying here one minute longer. I'm going to get my things. I want to go back. Rebie may be there——'

Trelawney let her talk, his expression enigmatic, and then as she was about to turn away he asked her, '*Aren't* I safe, Daisy?'

'What do you mean?'

'I mean, are you going to tell Rebie? About us,' he added pithily.

Meaning by *that*, that she'd co-operated. But she'd explained why, she thought wildly. He knew it had nothing to do with him. And why on earth should he imagine she'd tell *anyone* what had happened, let alone Rebie? Head up, she looked straight at him, and felt her legs turn to water. Why hadn't she wrenched herself away from him? She could have, even if she'd had to punch him in the chest, where she knew it would hurt. Now the way he was looking at her made her feel terribly naked. There was an expression in his eyes that said he knew all there was to know about her—an expression that meant he had stripped her down to her very soul, until there was no feminine mystery left. It sent a shiver up and down her spine. Her thoughts were getting out of control. She could still feel the pressure of his hands on her buttocks, still feel his mouth moving against hers, and she knew that everything had changed in those few seconds they had been so close together. He was no longer a man years and years older than she was, a man whose adult sexual life was way outside her sphere of experience. Suddenly he'd come suffocatingly close—dragged her halfway into his own world——

But to think she'd run back to Jackalass and tell!

'What kind of a person do you think I *am*?' she breathed.

He looked at her hard before he answered.

'I think you're a woman like any other woman, Daisy. Though I don't pretend to be able to follow the devious workings of the female mind. God knows I try, but just when I think I have the answer, I'm baffled again. Experience seems no use. So I'm interested to know if you plan any action. You spread the news of my misdemeanours once before, didn't you?

'What?' she said blankly. She hadn't the least idea what he was talking about, and her golden hazel eyes were puzzled.

'Oh, come on,' he said impatiently. 'I don't hold it against you, but you surely haven't forgotten that night on the upstairs verandah when I asked you to keep my sleep-walking habits to yourself.'

Dale bit her lip. Of course she hadn't forgotten. That humid night in December when she and Rebie had been sleeping on the verandah, and she'd been kept awake by the lightning dancing across the sky and by the mournful call of the mopoke that had been so much in accord with her mood. Because soon she had to leave Jackalass and the Vinings and go back to her father and his new wife.

She'd heard the soft sound of a door closing, and she'd sat up instinctively, thinking it might be Aunt Beth. A dark shadow had moved towards her—a torch had shone in her eyes making her recoil, and Trelawney's voice, low and compulsive, had said, 'Lie down and go back to sleep, Daisy. You've been having a dream—so don't go spreading it around that I walk in my sleep.'

She had lain down, puzzled, as the torch went out and he disappeared silently. She'd heard Rebie murmur in her sleep and turn over, and she'd thought of what Trelawney had said. She hadn't been dreaming—and he hadn't been walking in his sleep. That door she'd heard closing—had it been the door of Arnoldine's room? Had he been—kissing Arnie? She didn't know, and somehow she didn't want to think about it. Not for anything would she say a word about it. If she mentioned it to Rebie, it would be passed on to somebody, because Rebie could never keep anything to herself, she was the greatest gossip of all time——

'Remember?' Trelawney said now.

'Yes,' she said slowly, uneasily, 'I remember. But I did keep it to myself that you'd been—sleepwalking.'

He laughed briefly. 'Oh no, you didn't, darling. David told me the next night he was going to give Arnoldine the sack. And to put a stop to that, I packed up and left myself. It wasn't hard to guess who'd been telling tales of course.'

'But I didn't!' she protested. 'I—I didn't even know what it was all about. You said you were walking in your sleep——'

'Good God, Daisy, you certainly didn't believe that! You knew damned well what it was all about—well enough to let Rebie in on it. Only the other day the subject came up and she happened to say you'd said you were going to tell her father. Not that any of it matters now.'

Oh, it wasn't true, what Rebie had said! But Dale could hardly say so—not when Trelawney was engaged to Rebie. Rebie must have been awake—told tales herself. And shifted the blame on to Dale. Not every pleasant. . . . She shrugged and kicked up some sand with her bare feet. Let him believe what he liked, she thought, and told him, 'Well, whatever you think—it's rather miserable to blame it on a child of eleven when—when after all, you were the one who was——' she paused, rejected 'making love to the governess', and said instead, 'in the wrong. Anyhow, I guess Uncle David knew what was going on.'

'Okay,' he said equably, but his eyes were hard. 'Let's forget it. But if you have it in mind to tell Rebecca I made a pass at you, let me know, will you?'

'So you can get in first and blame it on me?' she flashed, and he uttered a short cynical laugh.

'I might get away with that too,' he said softly, his glance raking over her trembling body. 'Most girls out here don't wear swimming gear like yours, you know. They cover up. You're pretty close to naked—something I hardly expected when I suggested we revisit the haunts of your childhood.'

Dale's face had gone pale, though inwardly she was boiling with rage and resentment. How dared he talk to her like that? She hated him now for kissing her—hated herself for allowing it, even though she hadn't known then about him and Rebie. He was altogether detestable, she decided, and Rebie was mad to get engaged to him. She said through her teeth, 'You needn't worry, Trelawney Saber. I wouldn't be bothered making a fuss about your—your measly little kiss!'

She saw his eyes narrow and his nostrils dilate, and for a second she thought he was going to pay her out for that remark. She turned away swiftly and began to run. Trelawney didn't follow her, and she reached the clothes she'd dropped on the ground and swooped on them. Her bikini was bone dry by now, and her short hair was standing on end. She dragged on the black jeans, the black vest, while he stood down near the water watching her.

'Are you coming?' she shouted at him, then climbed into the car—*her* car—and saw with satisfaction that the keys were still in the ignition. She switched on, got the motor going, made it roar. Imagine having to go back to a house where there was no one but him and her! Though perhaps Rebie might be there by now. *His fiancée.*

Suddenly her longing for Rebie's arrival seemed to have disappeared. It would no longer be a case of herself and Rebie catching up on old times, talking nineteen to the dozen, renewing their childhood friendship. It would be all Rebie and Trelawney. *He'd* be monopolising her—making love to her—despite his broken ribs. Dale would be the odd man out, left on her own, unless the visitors came back too. That at least would make it more bearable.

On top of these tumbled thoughts, as she sat there, the motor racing, and Trelawney, hands in pockets, came sauntering towards her, came another. Illogical, yet somehow satisfying. *This* was why Rebie hadn't come hastening back to be with him. He was so *odious*. Who'd ever want to rush in and get tied up with him? She was probably regretting the engagement already.

She glared at him as he reached the car. Then instead of going round to the passenger side, he stopped near her, turned the handle and wrenched open the door. She should have driven off and left him, she thought, alarmed despite herself at the look on his face. It would have taught him a lesson—if Trelawney Saber *could* be taught a lesson, that was.

'Get your foot off the accelerator and move over,' he

commanded. 'I'm driving.'

'No, you're not—it's my car.'

'And right now you're not fit to drive it,' he grated. 'Your bad temper's boiling over, and I have no intention of being shaken to death.'

'My bad temper!' she exploded, hanging on to the wheel and refusing to move.

'Yes, your *foul* temper,' he enlarged. 'It's no wonder your boy-friend left you. You're a really savage little piece of work when you're roused.'

Tears of anger flew to her eyes. He certainly didn't believe in pouring oil on troubled waters! 'I'm not half as savage as you,' she flared. 'You think you can insult me all you like—tell me all my faults—and that I'll just meekly take it all. Well, I won't. I dislike you *intensely*, and if I even began to tell you what I thought of you—you'd—you'd——'

'Oh, I'd pretty soon find some way of quietening you down,' he said, his glittering eyes going to her mouth. 'And at the risk of adding fuel to the fire, let me tell you it's my opinion that girls who run away from their own tangled lives shouldn't bring their grievances with them. You as good as told me I got my just deserts in having to leave Jackalass. Well, I should say the same principle applies in your case. I'll enlarge on it, if you like.'

'I don't like,' she said furiously, and put her hands over her ears.

'Good. Then shift your bottom along that seat and be quick about it, or I'll give you a helping hand.'

For a split second Dale considered pretending she couldn't hear him, but it was for a split second only. He wouldn't hesitate to move her bodily, and much as she disliked him, the thought of what that might do to his ribs made her shudder inwardly. She took her hands away from her ears and edged over, and didn't even turn her head as he eased himself in behind the wheel. At least he didn't underline his victory. He merely slammed the door and got the car moving.

She sat beside him and ignored him, too angry to enjoy the lovely colours of the light and the landscape as the sun went down. As she calmed down a little, she tried to get her thoughts into some sort of logical order. It hurt to be called bad-tempered, because she wasn't—she really wasn't. 'No wonder your boy-friend left you,' he said, but Andrew hadn't dropped her because she was bad-tempered. He'd dropped her because he thought she was cold-blooded. For a freezing instant she wondered why it was she hadn't hated *him* for telling her that. But the answer was simple, of course. You can't hate someone when you love them, and he'd misunderstood her apparent cold-bloodedness. Thank goodness she hadn't told Trelawney anything about that! If he thought she'd slept with Andrew, then let him think it. She didn't care. He was contemptible, anyhow. He had no right to touch her—kiss her —when he was engaged to another girl. And then to suggest she might tell! His implication that she'd worn her bikini to provoke him was just the last straw. But no—she amended that. The last straw was having him call her bad-tempered. All in all, it was no wonder she was in such a turmoil.

She stole a look at him sitting silently beside her, his eyes on the uneven track he was following across the paddock. She felt a foolish pang of guilt because—because he had been injured, and she shrugged it off impatiently. She wasn't going to feel sorry for him. Her glance lingered on the tawny hair that lay across his forehead, on the line of his cheek, curving in from the high cheekbone. The scar was on the other side of his face, so she couldn't see it.

How had he got that scar? she wondered, a little disconcerted at the way her thoughts were wandering.

Neither of them had said a word and now they were nearly back at the homestead. Dale decided she'd have to say something—get some semblance of normality back between them. It wouldn't do to be so obviously strained if Rebie—and maybe the guests—should have arrived.

'Trelawney——'

He didn't turn his head. 'Well?'

'I was wondering—how did you get that scar on your face?'

'What?' He looked at her in surprise, and smiled suddenly. 'Good God, that happened way back—when I was twelve or so and came into rather unpleasant contact with a steer. I was working in the holding yard and I was just a bit slow in getting up on the rails. It sure taught me the virtue of knowing how—and when—to move fast.'

'Where was that?' she asked, a little shocked that such a thing should happen to so young a child.

'At Warathar.'

'Did you live there when you were a child? Was your father the manager then?'

He didn't answer straight away, and then he told her, 'Well, I started life here but my father never reached the stage of being manager, though it was the general idea. You see, my mother died when I was born, and my father got out and joined the permanent air-force. I lived with my grandfather on the Darling Downs property. But somehow or other my roots were always here—the Sabers took up the run in 1890. As soon as I was old enough I used to come here for holidays—Ray was here by that time, he was a lot younger than my father. The old man encouraged it, of course—he didn't want me to opt out of the cattle industry the way my father had.'

'Oh,' Dale said slowly, her mind turning over what he had said. 'And your father—did he marry again?'

'No. He was killed in a training manoeuvre when I was six or so.'

Dale wanted to say she was sorry, but she didn't. He wouldn't want her to. But all the same she was sorry, and at the back of her mind she felt it all had something to do with his being the way he was. Hard—callous. That was how she saw him, anyhow. There'd been no woman —no mother-figure—no softening influence in his life. Unless perhaps his grandmother——

'Your grandmother helped bring you up, I suppose,' she said slowly.

'My grandmother died before I was born,' he said, and added dryly, 'In fact, there were no women in my early life. Are you thinking it—shows?'

She turned away from him. 'Yes, I think it does.'

He said nothing.

CHAPTER FOUR

REBIE wasn't there, when they arrived back at the homestead. No one was there, just herself and Trelawney. And she knew it couldn't go on. The whole situation had changed quite drastically. Apart from the fact that he had made a pass at her, there were other reasons why she couldn't feel anything like comfortable with him again. She didn't like the fact that he thought of her as a talebearer—— Well, if it isn't little Daisy Driscoll, the kid who put me in and practically had me kicked out of Jackalass. First impressions stick, and he wouldn't be likely to trust her now. It was a nasty feeling.

Then she wished she hadn't let him pressure her into telling him about Andrew. As from now, she was keeping quiet about herself, and she'd have no more to do with him than was absolutely necessary.

She cooked dinner—which he took for granted—serving him steak and the fresh vegetables Fred had brought into the kitchen while they were away. Afterwards, over the washing up, she did some thinking. Trelawney had gone to sit outside in the cooler night air, but she wasn't going to join him—not that he'd asked her to, as a matter of fact. Anyhow, she was going early to bed, and if it killed her she'd be sound asleep hours before he came up. She didn't even want to hear him come up the stairs—she didn't want to know he was there. She wanted to shut herself right off from him.

But before she went up to bed there was something she was going to tell him. It was no use brooding, waiting, smouldering. She was going to take action.

She let the screen door swing to with a sharp sound as she went outside so he'd know she was coming and she wouldn't have to say his name. He looked round, expectantly, she thought, and then stood up, and she wondered if he thought she'd come to make her peace with him— maybe to apologise. For what, she wasn't sure, but if she had something to apologise for, then so had he.

'I'm going out to the muster camp tomorrow,' she said, standing a few feet away from him under the mango trees. 'And in case you're suspicious, it's not to tell Rebie any tales,' she added rapidly, getting in first.

'About my measly little kisses, you mean,' he said, and deliberately let his glance trail from her eyes to her mouth, and then to her breast and her hips.

Her heartbeats quickened nervously.

'That's right,' she agreed. 'I'm tired of hanging about here, waiting for Rebie—tidying up—cooking your meals——'

'I believe you're trying to tell me something,' he said when she paused. 'Such as that I'm in your debt, and not suitably appreciative. Is that it? I gather you plan to leave me on my own, to settle for sleeping under the stars at the muster camp.'

Dale shook her head. She had no intention of doing that. It just didn't appeal, here and now.

'I'll get Rebie to come back with me. You shouldn't be on your own.'

'Shouldn't I? Well, it's nice of you to be so considerate, Daisy, but being alone wouldn't bother me in the slightest,' he said coolly. 'If it did, I could have someone come over from Warathar to drive me back there. However, I don't plan to do that. Like you, I'm waiting for Rebecca. And since you're going to the muster I'll come along with you.'

'Why?' she said, taken aback. 'To make sure I don't cause trouble?'

'To make sure you don't get *into* trouble,' he corrected her. 'You could very easily get lost, you know. It's happened before this.'

Dale was disconcerted. That was something she hadn't thought about. But she said carelessly, 'I'd be all right. Only I suppose you want to see Rebie too. Well, I suppose you can come. I'll be leaving in the morning, straight after breakfast.'

'That will suit me fine,' he said irritatingly. He indicated a chair. 'Won't you sit down? Then we can continue talking in comfort.'

'There's nothing more to say,' Dale said coldly. 'Goodnight. I'll see you in the morning.' She turned and went swiftly inside. She hadn't told him she was going to bed.

She had an uneasy feeling that to mention bed could be to invite some crack from him.

Upstairs, she didn't switch on her light until she'd closed her door, and then she got to bed as quickly as she could. She'd used the bathroom downstairs, and she calculated Trelawney wouldn't know where she was. She lay in the hot darkness longing to open her door, and longing still more to be able to sleep on the verandah. Well, tomorrow night Rebie would be here, and perhaps the Richards too, and all this trauma would be over.

She paid particular attention to her appearance next morning. She didn't want Rebie to suspect even for the fraction of a second that Trelawney Saber might have been tempted to kiss her, and so the drearier she looked the better. She wore black jeans and the saggiest of her shirts —and it was remarkable just how saggy it was. Of course, it was old, and as well she'd lost weight since the break-up with Andrew. She chose the black and white jogging shoes in preference to her black sandals, and then had a look at herself in the mirror. Her usually fair skin had suffered from its exposure to the sun yesterday and was decidedly pink, and her small nose was shiny. As for her hair, all the copper glitter had gone by now, and it was pale and uninteresting. She was tempted to find scissors and tidy up the cut a little, but what did it matter? The worse she looked the better it would serve her purpose. She brushed her hair hard and pushed what she could of it back behind her ears, with the result that she looked rather like a truant schoolgirl.

When she went downstairs, Trelawney's glance at her was one of distaste. He'd been in the kitchen and he'd cooked breakfast—for her as well as for himself, she discovered a little uncomfortably. He obviously assumed she resented having to cook for him from what she'd said last night, and she felt ashamed. She should have been a little more dignified, she thought. She didn't mind cooking, and would certainly far sooner do it herself than have him do it for her. He must have wakened early to be up before her, and she wondered how late he had been going to bed, for she hadn't heard a sound before she went to sleep. He was looking haggard again, too.

'Didn't you sleep well?' she asked, as he put a plate of steak and eggs in front of her—far more than she wanted, but she refrained from protesting. She'd just have to eat it and shut up.

'Oh, I slept as well as I expected to,' he said carelessly. 'I hope you had a good night. At least I didn't hear you weeping. I told you you'd find talking therapeutic.'

Dale ignored the remark and began to eat her breakfast, and he sat down opposite her.

'Where is the muster camp?' she asked after a little while.

He narrowed his eyes. 'Will it mean anything to you if I say it's out beyond the Coppertops?'

'Not very much,' she admitted reluctantly. 'I—I seem to remember the Coppertops are hills——'

'Ironstone ridges,' he agreed. 'But if you don't know where they are, don't let it bother you. I'll see we get there safely. I put some more petrol in your tank last night, by the way—we don't want to be stranded.'

'No. I suppose Rebie will come back in my car, won't she?'

'Why not?' he said agreeably.

'And the others—the Richards—do you think they'll come too?'

'I wouldn't know. I've met them only briefly—they're brother and sister—Philippa and Ivor, for your information. I think I told you they're from the city and keen to get an eyeful of outback life. They just might prefer to stay on with the muster ... Oh, another thing—I've arranged for a couple of girls to come in to do the washing up and clean the place up a bit, so you won't have a thing to do.'

He looked straight at her as he spoke, and her eyes fell, but all the same she felt a spark of annoyance. He *wanted* to embarrass her. He was picking her up on every single thing she'd said last night. She said icily, 'I don't think you should have done that since there'll be no one here to supervise the girls.'

'Don't worry, they're very reliable. Lila is Mission-trained—she's been working here for three or four years.' He stood up as he spoke. 'Let me know when you're ready to leave.'

To her surprise, when she went out to the car some twenty minutes later, he was leaving the driving to her.

'Aren't you afraid my incompetence—coupled with my bad temper—will give you an uncomfortable ride?' she asked cynically.

'No, darling. I think you're going to drive very carefully,' he said seriously.

Dale looked at him suspiciously. He had stretched one arm along the back of the seat behind her shoulders, and he was surveying her quizzically.

'I don't know why you should be so confident about that,' she said, mainly to cover up the shock that had gone through her as she met his blue-green eyes at such close quarters. 'I told you yesterday how I felt about you. You might suspect I could be spiteful, as well as being a—an informer.'

'No, I don't think you're spiteful, Daisy,' he said thoughtfully, as she started up the motor. 'If you were, you'd have had something catty to say about this girl your ex-boy-friend's taken up with. And you haven't said a word.'

'Oh, don't worry—I hate her,' Dale said bitterly from her heart.

'You know her?'

'No. I only saw her once—when she came into the shop to meet Andrew. After we'd parted.' She shut off anything more she might have said. She hadn't meant to tell him another thing, and here she was, opening up, answering his questions. He seemed to have some special ability to make her talk when she didn't want to. She changed the subject deliberately. 'I suppose driving yesterday didn't do you any good. You look——'

'Old?' he suggested when she hesitated. 'Well, I feel old when I look at you. You look fifteen at the most today, a schoolgirl, not a young woman going through the trauma of losing her lover to someone else. However, to come back to me—it wasn't the driving that threw me. It was—kissing you better. So if you like you can say it served me right, under the circumstances—and if I want to make something of it, I can say damn you, Daisy, for leading me into it.'

'I didn't lead you into it,' she said angrily, wondering if he were preparing his defence just in case she hinted at his behaviour to Rebie. Her attention had momentarily been diverted from what she was doing and the car gave a sudden lurch. She felt stricken.

Trelawney said ironically, 'Don't look so anguished— as if you've all but killed the thing you love. I'm still alive and kicking. All the same, I think we'll concentrate on the one thing. No more talking.'

Thank heavens for that, Dale thought. Talking to Trelawney seemed only to get her back up. From then on she gave all her attention to the track, and to his occasional directions when the wheel tracks simply disappeared. They were driving through reddish Flinders grass now. Occasionally a big red kangaroo bounded across the flat or stood motionless, scarcely discernible among the giant anthills scattered through the open forest of ironbarks and bloodwoods. A butcher bird warbled sweetly, a topknot pigeon flew in among the pale green leaves of a gidgee, tipping its tail up and balancing delicately on a branch. The day was shimmeringly hot, and ahead ironstone ridges stood out against the skyline. Those must be the Coppertops, she thought. Beyond them was the muster camp, and at the muster camp she'd be meeting Rebie and Kevin again. And wouldn't they be surprised to see her! Pleasantly, she hoped. She thought sadly about Aunt Beth and wished in vain that she'd come back here for a visit long ago. But regrets are futile. The only thing to do was to hang on to her happy memories and be content with that.

It was strange how the sounds and smells of the muster camp came back as, some time later, on the other side of the ridges, she caught sight of the camp. The dust—like a cloud of red smoke. The smell of it—and the bellowing of the cattle. The once familiar sight of the ringers in their curly-brimmed hats and checked shirts and tight trousers——

As they drove down to the camp, a stream of cattle was coming slowly in to join the mob already yarded, and over near the big truck the cook was busy getting midday dinner for the hungry men. Dale couldn't see Rebie or the other girl, Philippa, as she pulled up in the shade of a big ironbark and stared out, her eyes narrowed against the glaring sunlight. She couldn't see Kevin either—or anyone who looked as if he might be Kevin.

Trelawney had swung open his door.

'Wait here, Daisy, I'll ask one of these characters where

everyone is. You can bet your bottom dollar Rebie at least won't be out in the scrub riding after the cattle. She's sure to be around somewhere.'

She watched him stride off in the direction of the supplies truck, where he stopped and spoke to the cook, a big man with his hat on the back of his head and brawny arms showing beneath rolled-up shirt sleeves. Some of the stockmen who'd just come in with the cattle stared in her direction, and presently Trelawney came back.

'Rebecca's down at the creek. The other two are taking part in the muster. Hop out, Daisy—we'll go and hunt Rebie up.'

Dale left the shade of the car somewhat apprehensively. She'd brought the beat-up old straw hat she'd found in the house, and now she crammed it on her head and refused to check up on Trelawney's reaction to the sight she must now present. When she'd left Rockhampton she'd been quite certain she didn't care a fig how she looked. In her mind it had been a pilgrimage back to childhood. It was only since then that she'd found there was no road back, and now she knew it would have been more worthy of her, more dignified, to have brought her normal clothes. Still, there really was some point in her looking like a foundling today. She didn't want Rebie getting ideas about what might have happened in the time she'd been alone with her fiancé.

She was feeling distinctly nervous as they approached the gums that grew along by the creek, and when she half stumbled, Trelawney put a hand under her elbow. She drew away from him sharply, as if she'd been bitten by a bull ant.

'Okay,' he said irritably. 'But for God's sake stop tottering along as if each step is the last one you're capable of taking. What is there to be so nervous about? I thought you were looking forward to seeing Rebecca.'

'I am. My legs are cramped,' Dale lied. It would have been so much easier to have turned up on her own instead of with—him. 'Has Rebie changed much?' she asked aloud.

'In ten years? I should hope so,' he said dryly. 'But you can judge for yourself in a minute—there she is. Trust Rebie to come equipped with a lounger,' he added amusedly.

Dale followed his glance through the trees. Some distance ahead she could see a girl sprawling on a folding lounger, the brim of a hat, the colour of crushed strawberries, hiding her face. She was reading, and quite unaware of their approach.

'Do you want to go and surprise her?' Trelawney asked.

Dale hesitated. He made it sound childish, and in fact she wasn't really sure he was serious, yet—why not? Wasn't it just what she did want to do?

'It would be fun,' she said.

'Then go ahead. I'll stay out of the way,' he said agreeably.

Dale very nearly asked, 'Aren't you afraid I might tell tales?' but she refrained. There was no point in harping on it, and if he was willing to let her get together with Rebie without his being present, then he must trust her. He probably thought he'd scared her into complying, anyhow, with his threats of blaming everything on her.

Trelawney turned back, and she went on, her jogging shoes making no sound on the sandy creek bank. Besides the strawberries-and-cream hat, Rebie wore a matching blouse, white shorts, and high-heeled white sandals. Her legs were long and slender, and so far Dale could see little resemblance to the plump little dumpling of ten years ago.

A twig cracked under her feet, and the girl on the

lounger looked up and stared. Dale stared too. *Was* it Rebie? It must be—Trelawney had said so. But oh, how she had changed! The glasses were gone—yet she'd been reading! Her face was no longer round, and her eyes were a beautiful sparkling blue. She was, in fact, a superlatively attractive girl. Suddenly it no longer seemed impossible that she should be engaged to Trelawney. Dale smiled hesitantly, newly conscious of her own far from prepossessing appearance.

'Hello, Rebie.' She said it almost shyly.

Rebie slid her feet to the ground and stood up. A look of comical dismay crossed her face briefly before she sent Dale a wide friendly smile that showed good teeth.

'Daisy!' she exclaimed incredulously. 'It can't be! Where on *earth* did you spring from all of a sudden?'

Where did she look as if she'd sprung from? Dale wondered wryly. She pulled the battered hat from her head and pushed her hair back from a forehead that was damp with perspiration.

'You've been to Jackalass,' Rebie said. 'That old hat of Mother's.' She stopped, her face sobering, and Dale said quietly, 'I heard about Aunt Beth—Trelawney told me. I'm so terribly sorry, I had no idea. I thought—I thought I'd find you all still here.'

'Oh no, we're not all here by any means. The whole set-up's changed. But when did you come? Come and sit down—let's talk.' Rebie looked across Dale's shoulder. 'Is Trelawney with you?' she demanded, her voice sharpening.

'Yes. But don't worry, I did the driving,' Dale said reassuringly. 'His ribs are—well, he has to take things quietly. Very quietly,' she added so Rebie wouldn't miss the point.

'His ribs?' Rebie echoed. She sat down on the lounger. 'What do you mean—his ribs?'

Dale, sitting down too, stared at her, feeling puzzled.

'Why, he broke them—cracked them—the other day. When he was here at the muster camp.'

'*Did* he?' The other girl's face had flushed. 'Good lord! I knew that horse threw him—and I was in a bit of a panic when it happened, with no one else around. But—well, he got straight back into the saddle, so I presumed he was all right. He *is*, isn't he?'

'Well, yes. He's got his chest strapped up, but he can't do anything in the least strenuous, as you might imagine —not with a few broken bones.'

'I suppose not,' Rebie agreed, then discarded the subject to ask, 'When did you arrive, Daisy?'

'A couple of days ago,' Dale admitted reluctantly, wishing she could have said, This morning. 'He—Trelawney— was in bed asleep when I turned up. It was late, and I thought the house was deserted. It was stupid of me not to contact you and ask if it was okay to come, but I did it more or less on impulse.'

'Well, you don't have to stand on ceremony with us, Daisy. But you might have known we'd be out at the muster. Yet I suppose you'd have thought Mother would be there. Someone should have let you know she was ill, but we thought you'd moved when you didn't write at Christmas. And then we were all pretty shattered when we found just how ill she really was—I guess no one thought of anything much but her. The doctor gave her six months at the most, you see, but Daddy bought this place near Charters Towers. The climate's good there, and besides, he wanted to be near the hospital when she had to go. Kev took over here, as you probably know.'

'Yes. Trelawney told me.'

'Yes, well, Buff's looking after Daddy now, so I thought I'd come and keep an eye on Kev. Heaven knows, I'm not a good housekeeper, but I'd been thinking of leaving my job, and as a matter of fact, I really didn't like the fact that there was such a dearth of females here.' She sent Dale a knowing look from her incredibly lovely eyes. 'Did you know Arnie moved over to Warathar when it was obvious she couldn't stay on at Jackalass? At her own invitation, by the way. And I could just imagine her trying to boss the whole show—shuttling between there and the outstation. Has she been at Jackalass? Did Tree let her know he was there?'

'No, I don't think he did. She hasn't been there anyhow. Only——' Dale broke off enlarging on what seemed a slightly dangerous subject and asked instead, 'What was your job, Rebie?'

'Photographer's receptionist. Rather futile, but quite a bit of fun. Actually, I was learning a bit about portraiture, but I wasn't desperately keen. I seem to remember Mother saying you'd gone in for interior decorating.'

'Not exactly. I was with a decorating firm, but mostly I was making up orders—you know, doing curtains and chair covers and bedspreads and so on.'

'It's great to see you, anyhow. How long a holiday do you have?'

Dale spread her hands. 'I'm like you. I've left my job.'

'Oh, why? I'd have thought you'd enjoy it.'

'I did. But there were problems, with the people I worked for,' Dale explained clumsily.

'Sounds like man trouble,' Rebie said shrewdly. Then when Dale added nothing to what she'd already said, she asked, 'What brought you all this way here, anyhow?'

'Nostalgia,' Dale said after a second. In a way, that was true. The fact was, she didn't feel like giving her romantic troubles an airing just yet. It wasn't as if she and Rebie had kept closely in touch, and it suddenly struck her as odd that nothing had been said about Rebie's engagement to Trelawney. She said a little formally, 'Trelawney told me you and he are engaged.'

'Yes.' Rebie's smile was somehow wary. 'I'll bet you were suprised. It all happened rather quickly—only about a week ago, as a matter of fact. I haven't really got used to it yet. I was quite sure Arnie would grab him after Buff left, but he asked *me* to marry him. She's as mad as a hornet, of course. I always suspected she came outback in the first place to find herself a cattleman, and there she is, going on for forty, and she hasn't managed it yet! Do you remember what a hot line she was doing with Trelawney when we were kids? And when Daddy found out, he sent *him* away, when it would have been better sense to get rid of her.' She grimaced. 'Men are funny, aren't they? So then she just stayed and stayed, even after Joanne had gone away to school.'

'I thought she stayed to help Aunt Beth,' Dale said uncomfortably. She couldn't help remembering at this point that Rebie had let Trelawney think *she* had told Uncle David about him and the governess.

'Well, that was the story,' Rebie said with a shrug. 'She was probably hoping Trelawney would come back, if you ask me. Oh, she's quite a good housekeeper,' she admitted grudgingly, 'and Daddy and Mother had got used to having her around the place. But I could never stand her, not even at the very start.'

'I didn't know that,' Dale said thoughtfully. She thought uneasily of all the tricks they'd played on Arnie under Rebie's leadership. They'd seemed harmless enough to her then, but perhaps Rebie had taken a delight in tormenting the woman she didn't like. And now she was delighted to have snatched Trelawney from under her very nose. Or was that uncharitable? Because surely she must be in love with him. An odd thought floated into her mind—that he was the kind of man with whom one could fall in love quite dementedly. *She* couldn't, of course, because she didn't even like him, but——

'Didn't you really?' Rebie was saying laughingly. 'I thought everyone knew Arnie and I were like oil and water. Maybe the animosity stems from the day she tried to get us to learn "I love a sunburnt country", and when I refused she told me I should be ashamed—that I had no feeling for my land and all that stuff. After that, I never agreed with anything she said ... where's Trelawney, anyhow? Has he gone out to find Kevin and the others?'

Dale shook her head. 'No driving, no riding.' Hadn't Rebie taken that in yet? Didn't she really know he'd been injured? 'He's somewhere about,' she went on, glancing around and wondering nervously if he'd heard any of their conversation. 'When the cook said you were down at the creek, I thought I'd give you a surprise.'

'You certainly did that! And honestly, Daisy, you look so young—such a kid still! Years and years younger than me. And so—so——'

'So frightful,' Dale said with a grimace. How to explain her rather ghastly appearance? 'These clothes are the only things I had for the bush, and my hair—well, I got so hot driving that I had it cut in some little one-horse town—don't ask me the name of it.'

'Don't worry, I won't,' Rebie said with a laugh. 'The result's definitely not a recommendation, to be quite frank.'

'No, it isn't, is it? ... Your eyes, Rebie—you used to wear glasses. Don't you need them now?'

'Sure I need them, but I wear contact lenses—the new soft ones. They're fabulous.' She glanced at the gold watch on her wrist. 'It's getting on for lunch time. Shall we go back? The others will be looking for us. I'll leave the lounger here. This is the coolest place to be, and I'm really lazy, lying about reading. But I hate riding in the dust and the heat.'

They strolled along the creek bank together and presently Trelawney came in sight. As they drew near, Rebie moved forward and raised her face for his kiss, and Dale turned away feeling oddly embarrassed.

'Tree, I hope you weren't annoyed when I didn't come back to see if that fall had affected you. It's such a long way, and I was sure you'd be all right—and anyhow, you've had Daisy to look after you, haven't you?' She looked at Dale and Trelawney looked at her too, sharply, sardonically, in a way that made her drop her eyes.

'Sure,' he said, his eyes still on Dale. 'Daisy's been doing a wonderful job. However, I've arranged for Lila to come over and clear up.'

'Oh—but why?' Rebie put in. 'I thought you and Daisy had come out to camp with us. You're surely not going back to Jackalass today!'

'Rebie, in my present state, I'm useless here. Moreover, I'm not going to sleep on the ground.' They had all begun to walk in the direction of the camp. 'I've broken a rib or two. Remember?'

'*Remember?*' Rebie repeated a little sulkily. I didn't know you'd broken your ribs till Daisy told me so just now. I thought you were joking about it the other day when you got up on your horse and rode off into the sunset. I expected you back next day, in fact. I've been *waiting* for you,' she went on, warming to her theme. 'Down by the creek, all on my own——'

'Have you?' He didn't apologise. 'Well, now you know why I didn't come and why I'm not staying now. How about you coming back with us instead? Daisy is counting on it. Aren't you, Daisy?'

'Oh, Daisy *darling*!' Rebie exclaimed. 'I can't—I really can't. It's just not possible. Philippa can't stay here without me, and she's Kev's very special guest, if you know what I mean. I can't just disappear and leave her in a camp full of men.'

'How about giving some thought to the fact that Daisy's a guest too?' Trelawney suggested dryly.

'Oh, but she's not,' Rebie protested. 'Daisy's family—she's quite different, even though we haven't seen her in years ... No, I can't come, and that's all about it. And after all, Tree, you were supposed to be here with us. I didn't know Daisy was coming, so she'll either have to get her things and come back or——' She paused, and looked assessingly at Trelawney. 'You do look frightful, Tree. Will you mind very much looking after him, Daisy? We'll be back soon, I'm sure. The others won't want to see the muster out.'

Dale bit her lip. If Rebie knew what Trelawney had been up to she wouldn't be so blithely handing him over into her care. But she never would know—and it wasn't going to happen again. And if protesting was likely to arouse her suspicions, then Dale wasn't going to protest. Not that she wanted to go back to the old set-up tonight, when she had come here specifically to bring Rebie back with her——

They had left the belt of trees by now and the camp was in sight. It looked as if midday dinner was just about ready. The stockmen had come in and were dismounting, and among them, almost instantly, she recognised Kevin—broad-shouldered, blue-eyed, with the same wide mouth as Rebie, though his hair was darker than hers. Funnily enough, he looked at her as she strolled across with the others and recognised her as quickly as she had recognised him, and it made her feel good. He paused to call out to a tall girl in brown slacks and fawn shirt, one long fair braid hanging over her shoulder from under a smart brown cap. Philippa, she thought, and noticed even from a distance how much at home the other girl seemed at the muster camp. She fitted in absolutely. Rebie, on the other hand, didn't, which was unexpected in a way. Her strawberries and cream didn't belong in this setting. To tell the truth, Dale knew that even *she* looked more part of the scenery than Rebie did. Yet it was still Rebie who belonged here, by birth and upbringing. And it was Rebie who was going to marry Trelawney Saber—live at Warathar, be missus to his boss, bring up her children in this particular part of the outback.

Dale pulled up her errant thoughts in mid-flight and looked at the third member of the little group that now came towards them like a welcoming party. Ivor—Philippa's brother—lighting a cigarette, blowing smoke, walking more slowly than the others.

'I can't believe it!' Kevin said a moment later, taking Dale's hand and looking down smilingly into her face. 'Daisy Driscoll! Lord, it's good to have you with us again!' He spoke as if she had come to stay and as if it were the most natural thing in the world. 'Mother would have loved this.'

'I'm so sorry I'm too late, Kevin,' said Dale, her voice choked. Strangely, though she hadn't known Kevin as well as the younger members of the family, she still had the feeling he was a brother. And as he bent his head and kissed her, she thought, tears starting to her eyes, that *he* knew what comforting meant.

He was still holding her hand in his when he said, 'I'm forgetting—you haven't met my friends. Philippa—Ivor—this is Daisy Driscoll, who lived with us years and years ago. She's a special kind of sister. Daisy—Pip and Ivor Richards.'

Greetings and acknowledgements occupied the next few moments, until Ivor said to Trelawney, 'We've been wondering where you'd got to.'

'Rebie didn't tell you I'd gone to Jackalass?' he asked dryly.

'Sure. But we expected you back.'

'It's no wonder he didn't come,' said Rebie, hanging on to Trelawney's arm but fluttering her lashes at Ivor. 'Daisy turned up.'

Ivor glanced at Dale, and then away again, and she thought. 'He's crossed *me* out—he knows I don't count.' She looked warily at Trelawney, who said levelly, 'Well, besides Daisy, I had a fall and discovered I'd broken a few ribs. It's put me at a disadvantage for a few days—hence my submission to Daisy's chauffeuring me out here today ... Well, are we going to eat? I'm damned hungry, though I've no right to be.'

Somewhat to Dale's surprise—for she had expected they'd be roughing it—a table had been set up under the trees, spread with a checked cloth, and laid with cutlery and glasses. So that while the ringers lounged about on the ground and ate from aluminium plates, the Vinings, the Richards, Trelawney and Dale sat on canvas stools and ate in style, even if their food was the same hearty fare. Dale noticed too that there were two tents under the trees, and concluded that the sleeping arrangements were not as primitive as was usual—at least for the guests, and certainly for Rebie too.

Lunch concluded, she declined to take a horse and ride out with the others. There didn't seem much point in it, particularly since Ivor had decided against spending the afternoon in the saddle. Whether Dale went or stayed,

Rebie and Trelawney still wouldn't be left together for a tête-à-tête. The result was that the four of them chattered more or less idly for an hour or so before Trelawney decided it was time to go back to Jackalass.

'Your chest's hurting,' said Rebie with a sort of affectionate accusation, and observing the expression on his face, Dale recalled his aversion to being fussed over by a mother hen. 'You'll take care of him, won't you, Daisy? See he doesn't do anything mad.'

Trelawney turned his back as though her attitude were just too irritating to be tolerated, and Dale noticed that Ivor was giving her a very knowing and very speculative look, so that she too turned her face aside.

'What on earth does he imagine we're going to get up to?' she asked herself desperately. 'Surely he can see that Trelawney's—harmless at present.' Yet in her own heart she knew that *that* didn't eliminate the presence of danger. Ivor knew it too—but Rebie didn't. Simply because Dale looked so frightful.

She jammed the straw hat back on her head and followed Trelawney to the car.

CHAPTER FIVE

ONCE they were well away from the camp, Dale said, 'I'm surprised you let Rebie stay.'

Trelawney was leaning back against the seat, his eyes half closed, and she didn't know if that was because he hadn't slept well or if it was because he was in pain or just plain bored—with her.

'Are you? Why?' He said it indolently.

'Oh, because you're the sort of man who likes to run things his own way,' she said.

'So that's how you sum me up. Well, I dare say it's a fairly accurate assessment. But you've forgotten something, haven't you? *You* were the one who was intent on dragging Rebie back to Jackalass. It wasn't my idea.'

She bit her lip, exasperated. She didn't know what to make of him, and she didn't know what he meant. Was he stating a simple fact, or was he implying something? And if he was implying something, what was it? 'Do you think he's planning to make another pass at you?' an inner voice asked mockingly.

She moved in her seat uneasily. Of course she didn't imagine any such thing. Couldn't she ascribe some honest, generous motives to Trelawney? Wasn't it quite possible he didn't want to put an end to Rebie's enjoying herself with the others out at the muster camp? Presumably Rebie was enjoying herself, though Dale had gathered that she spent most of her time at the creek, reading, and perhaps swimming. On her own.

Yet not always on her own. This afternoon at least she was going to have Ivor Richards' company.

Dale glanced at Trelawney quickly. Didn't he mind? Wasn't he at all jealous? Didn't he want to break that up— to take Rebie away? After all, Ivor Richards was a good-looking young man—and Rebie was a decidedly attractive girl. She turned her head again, meaning to ask him wasn't he jealous, but she didn't ask it after all. It could be stirring up a hornets' nest, and she didn't want to do that. Besides, she couldn't imagine that Rebie could possibly prefer Ivor Richards to Trelawney.

The aboriginal girls had tidied up the house so that it was spotless. In the kitchen there were fresh vegetables and meat, butter and milk. Dale cooked the evening meal and they ate it almost in silence. The house seemed emptier than it had been before, the isolation more pronounced. There were lines on Trelawney's face, dark shadows under his eyes, and she suspected he was in pain, but she didn't dare comment in case he told her she was fussing. Besides, it wouldn't do for her to fuss; it might seem possessive. She longed to suggest he should go to bed early, but she couldn't do that either, and while she washed up she tried to work out the best way to make it possible for him to go to bed early. She didn't know if she felt any awkwardness about their both sleeping upstairs, but she rather thought he took it for granted.

Finally, to make things easy, she decided to take a walk. It was a very warm night, and it wouldn't seem off, the only risk was Trelawney might offer to come with her. But she could put a stop to that.

When she went outside a short time later to where he was sitting in the dark, she told him flatly, 'I'm going for a walk. I want to do some thinking.'

'Go ahead,' he said agreeably. 'I don't need to warn you to watch out for snakes, do I? Keep out of the long grass and don't go scuffling through the gum leaves.'

'I'll be all right.' She hadn't actually thought of snakes, but she'd learned to take care years ago, and it was more or less second nature to her. 'I thought I'd better tell you so you won't be wondering where I am.'

'Thanks for the consideration, but I don't expect to be needing you,' he said dryly. 'As a matter of fact I'm going to have a whisky and go up to bed in a few minutes.'

'Oh.' With difficulty Dale stopped herself from asking if he was in pain, and told him instead with cutting coldness, 'Don't drink too much. And if you aren't sure of the extent of the damage you've done, why don't you see a doctor?'

He raised a laconic eyebrow. 'The doctor's a long way off. But never fear, I know exactly what I've done to myself. I've seen it happen to many a stockman. My bones are no different from anyone else's. They'll mend if I keep them strapped up ... You go and take your walk and forget about me.'

'That won't be hard,' she retorted. 'I wasn't exactly planning to think about *you*.' She moved off and he called after her softly through the darkness, 'Be sure you get all your tears shed before you come upstairs, won't you, darling?'

Darling! Dale didn't reply. That awful habit he had of calling her darling. Of course it meant nothing, but all the same she wished he wouldn't.

She had her walk, though actually she didn't go far. Among the trees by the waterhole she found an open stretch of ground where there'd be no danger of snakes, and there she stretched out on sand that was still warm from the sun. She didn't really have any thinking to do—not even about Andrew. There was no future in that. It was a conclusion she'd somehow reached without even realising it. She leaned back on her hands and listened to the night noises and tried to identify them. The little scufflings— the water noises—they were difficult. But the crickets, the frogs, the song of the willy wagtail—those were all sounds she had learned by heart years ago. She strained her ears to hear the mournful cry of the mopoke, a sound linked so emotively, for her at least, with the outback night. But she didn't hear it, and nor did she hear the howling of a dingo, though this was dingo country. It was one of the reasons men ran cattle instead of sheep out here. Fred had acquired a dingo pup once, she remembered—a pretty little thing that he called Warry. She didn't know what became of it —she must ask him about it some time.

With a yawn, she closed her eyes.

When she opened them again, her limbs were cramped, and the Southern Cross, scintillating in the Milky Way, had swung over towards the west. She stretched shudderingly and scrambled to her feet. The air had grown cooler and she had no real idea of the time, but for sure by now Trelawney would be well and truly asleep. He wouldn't be worrying about her. She began to walk quickly back to the house. The world was silent and empty, as empty as if no other person existed. Yet out beyond the Coppertops were Rebie and Kevin, the Richards and a number of stockmen. It was strange to think of Rebie out there, asleep in her tent, while here at Jackalass she, Dale Driscoll, hurried back to the house where Trelawney Saber lay asleep.

Suddenly she was afraid of her thoughts. It was even worse than thinking about Andrew.

Back at the house, Trelawney had left the light burning in the living room. She switched it off, pulled off her shoes, and carrying them made her way silently up the stairs in darkness. Trelawney's light was off and she stood listening for a moment, then went into Rebie's room, closed the door softly, and groped her way across the room to put on the lamp on the dressing table. Immediately she was confronted by her own reflection, and she stood staring at herself. The solitude of the night was still in her eyes and they looked dark and full of dreams. Her glance wandered to her black clothes and she frowned. By tilting the glass, she could see her figure to below her waist—shapeless in the shabby shirt that was now smudged with red sand. She dusted it off impatiently, and viewed with disfavour the tangle of her hair. Running her fingers through it, she admitted to herself that if she took a little trouble with it after she'd shampooed it, it needn't look quite so straight and unattractive. Maybe tomorrow——

She peeled off her shirt, and in her flesh-coloured bra she looked completely different. She thought of the other day at the pool—of Trelawney's hands on her breasts—of how he had spun her round and held her so close to him . . .

She wasn't in the least sleepy now. She was wide awake and restless, and after a second she crossed the room to open the wardrobe and look in at Rebie's clothes. Lots of blue things—to match her eyes, she thought. She pulled out a long cream skirt decorated with blue braid, a creamy lace top—and held them against her in turn, looking at herself in the mirror. How she wished she'd brought some of her own pretty clothes with her!

But what on earth was wrong with her? Why should she be so interested in her appearance? Suddenly disgusted with herself, she let the skirt and top slip to the floor and turned away from her reflection.

As she did so, there was a sharp rap on the door. Her heart stopped—jumped—raced.

'Daisy?' Trelawney's voice said.

She didn't know whether to answer or not, and she looked around her wildly and saw by the little clock on the bedside table that it was half past two. Heavens! She'd had no idea she was so late. If she didn't answer, Trelawney would probably think she was asleep and go away, she decided recklessly, and stood where she was, unmoving, scarcely breathing.

'Daisy?' Her name was repeated, and still she said nothing. But it wasn't as easy as that. The door handle turned gently, and in a moment he was standing in the doorway, taking in the whole scene—herself half undressed, in bra and black jeans, Rebie's clothes on the floor at her feet.

'You're not in bed!' he exclaimed. 'I heard you come up some little while ago. Why didn't you answer when I called out? I thought you'd gone to sleep with the light on.'

'Well, I hadn't,' she exclaimed furiously. 'And who—who asked you to come in?' she added angrily. She saw that he was barefooted, and above his dark pants, his torso was naked except for the rib belt. By the tousled state of his hair, he must have just got out of bed, and pulled on his pants to come to her room.

'Darling,' he said sardonically, 'I haven't come in. I merely opened the door—to switch off your light. A quite honourable intention, surely. You're quite decent, anyhow —far more so than you were at the pool the other afternoon ... I'm going downstairs to make a cup of tea. Do you want some?'

'No,' she snapped, and turned her back on him. There were tears of humiliation in her eyes as she heard the door click shut. What on earth must he think she'd been doing? she wondered, as she stopped and gathered up the clothes she'd dropped and put them back in the wardrobe. She wished now she hadn't made such a thing of his opening her door. He'd explained it logically enough.

About to unfasten her bra and get into her pyjamas, she changed her mind and reached for her shirt. She *was* thirsty—so why not have a cup of tea since he was making some? Wouldn't it at least partly cancel out her rather hysterical behaviour if she went downstairs and joined him as though nothing were wrong? And nothing *was* wrong, except that she didn't like people opening her door without her permission. Which brought her back to the fact that she should have answered when he called out.

He glanced round when she came into the kitchen, and wordlessly reached down another cup. She sat on a high stool and watched him get milk, sugar, and open the tea caddy.

'I decided I'd like some tea after all,' she said needlessly.

'I guessed that was why you came down,' he agreed. 'I didn't think it was for the company.'

'I'm sorry I woke you when I came in,' she said after a minute. His back was to her as he poured hot water into the teapot to warm it.

'You didn't,' he said. 'I'd been awake for some time. I was beginning to wonder what the hell had happened to you, as a matter of fact. I wasn't sure you hadn't thrown yourself into the lagoon.'

Dale was shocked. But perhaps he was joking, and in case he was she ignored the remark. He made the tea, brought the teapot to the table and sat down opposite her.

'I've been thinking about you, Daisy,' he said then, looking across at her. She felt her pulses jump, and she licked her upper lip nervously.

'Why?' she asked abruptly.

'God knows. You're certainly not my business. But you worry me. Could be because Beth isn't here any more ... Milk for you, or do you like it black?'

'Black, please.' There was a tremor in her voice. She wondered if she'd made a mistake in coming downstairs, after all. She didn't look at him as he poured her tea, then pushed the cup across the table to her. What had he been thinking about her? she wondered. But she wasn't going to ask him. He poured his own tea and while he spooned sugar into it she lifted her cup and looked at him quickly, almost furtively, over it. The drawn lines on his face had faded again, he looked virile, dynamic—and she was afraid of him. Her glance lingered on the curve of his lips and she felt her pulses racing as he raised his head and looked at her fully.

'I'm going to give you a bit of advice, Daisy,' he said conversationally.

'What—about?' she demanded, half nervous, half aggressive.

'What do you think? Your love life, of course.'

'I don't have a love life,' she said, her voice low. It occurred to her that this was an absolutely crazy conversation to be having at nearly three o'clock in the morning. What on earth would Rebie think if she knew her fiancé was sitting here talking to Daisy Driscoll about her love life, in the Jackalass kitchen, while she was asleep in her tent miles away?

She swallowed, then said slowly and carefully, 'Anyhow, I don't want to talk about that sort of thing.'

Trelawney smiled faintly. 'I'm not asking you to talk about it. I'm the one who's going to do the talking, darling.' He studied her through narrowed eyes and she had the feeling he was choosing his words. Advising her as Aunt Beth would have done? She couldn't see it—not coming from Trelawney Saber. She was thoroughly on edge by the time he resumed, 'You loved a man—you slept with him—he deserted you for someone else. Now you're presumably punishing yourself for your failure, and you're thoroughly unhappy. But try looking at it this way, Daisy— you've failed with one man, that's all. It's hardly a valid reason for opting out of your sex, or whatever it is you're doing, having your hair cut off and hiding your femininity under a scruffy old black shirt. You're still the same girl underneath—a little wiser, a little more experienced, that's all, and there are plenty more men in the world. Why don't you quit all this brooding and try again? Though quite frankly you're going to have a battle if you get around looking butch.'

Dale's cheeks were burning. She'd lost the opportunity to correct him and say she hadn't slept with Andrew, and besides, she hated talking about that sort of thing—par-

ticularly to Trelawney. As for brooding, she'd already
given that up. And though what he said probably made
sense, she didn't like the way he put it. Aunt Beth would
have had a far more sensitive approach. As for his saying
she looked butch, that was just a crude and deliberate ex-
aggeration.

'It doesn't matter how I look,' she said, her chin up.
'There's no one about except you.'

He raised his eyebrows. 'And I don't count?'

'No, of course not. Anyhow, you're engaged to Rebie.'

'And if I weren't?'

Her hand had begun to shake and she set down her cup.
The direction the conversation was taking was impossible,
and the sooner it ended the better.

'It wouldn't make any difference,' she assured him. I'm
not interested in—in men at all, not any more.'

She slipped off her stool, indicating the conversation was
over.

'Aren't you?' Trelawney stood up too, and as she moved
he stepped in front of her, his broad shoulders no more
than a foot away from her, his body blocking her way. She
knew he was going to take up her challenge—he would see
it like that—and at this minute she didn't see how she
could possibly stop him. She could try to dodge past him,
run for it—and that was about all. But she didn't do it.
She stayed where she was, breathing fast, and her gaze slid
over the rib belt to the wide bare brown band of flesh
above the top of his pants, then followed the dark gold
mat of hair that ran down his diaphragm to his navel. She
was aware that his breath had quickened almost as much as
hers had.

'I'm afraid I don't believe you, Daisy,' he said. 'You're
a healthy normal girl, and to be interested in men—in sex
—is so damned natural you'd have to be really sick to lose

your taste—particularly once you've indulged it.'

'Then maybe I am sick,' she said huskily. She was trembling all through, waiting for what must inevitably happen. She had no idea how she was going to react when he put his arms around her, his mouth on hers, but she was going to find out pretty soon, because she didn't have a hope in the world of escaping him.

'I doubt it,' he said. 'And I'd advise you to take to heart the advice I've given you.'

And then, instead of reaching out and pulling her to him as she had been quite certain he would do, he added harshly, 'Make yourself look like a woman, Daisy. That way, you'll be treated like one.' He raised his arm, but not to touch her. Instead, he indicated the door. 'Are you going up to bed?'

'Yes.' Dale said it quiveringly. Going, he'd said—not coming. She felt exactly as if she'd been slapped across the face, and she knew—she *knew*—that he'd been fully aware of what she'd expected. Fleetingly she remembered her own remark the other day about his measly little kiss. Was he remembering that too?—and paying her out for saying such a thing?

She slipped past him and out of the room, found her way to the stairs, and ran up them pantingly. She was glad he hadn't kissed her. She hadn't wanted it—she'd merely expected it, because she knew the kind of man he was—a man who liked to play around with women. Well, he wasn't going to play around with her. She didn't like him.

She paused at the top of the stairs. She could hear him in the room below and as he started up the stairs, she turned round and shouted down to him.

'I'd never want to look like a woman for *you*, Trelawney Saber! I said you don't attract me, and you'd better believe it. You're not so wonderful you can expect every girl you meet to fall in love with you!'

With that she fled, and for the second time she slammed her door shut.

As she stripped off her clothes she didn't even glance in the mirror. He'd said she looked butch. Well, great—she'd continue to look that way for his especial benefit. She switched off the light and got into bed.

Her tears, when she shed them, bitterly, weakly, stifling them with her face pressed into the pillow, weren't for Andrew and a love that was lost. She didn't know what they were for, unless she was crying from sheer emotional exhaustion...

It was so late when she woke the next day that the morning was nearly over. Thank goodness, she thought, remembering with a sick feeling in her stomach what had happened the night before. She wished now that she had held her tongue instead of shouting at him the way she had. It simply didn't bear thinking about, and she pushed it all to the back of her mind while she showered and dressed.

When she went downstairs the floors had been cleaned, the kitchen was tidy, Lila and Susie had gone, and Trelawney was nowhere to be seen. Dale wished that he'd gone back to Warathar, but somehow she didn't think he had. She cooked herself some scrambled eggs and made coffee, then worked out plans for making herself scarce. She might ask Fred to see about getting her a nice quiet pony. It would be a chance to brush up her doubtful horsemanship before the others came back. She hadn't done any riding for years, and she didn't want to be at a disadvantage.

Despite her late start, the day was long. She didn't ride far, she discovered she hadn't forgotten how it was done, and that it didn't keep her thoughts from troubling her. She stopped along by the creek, tethering her pony to a branch, and wishing the time away while she watched the birds and insects. No matter where she started, her thoughts returned persistently to last night and Trelawney's advice. She kept telling herself that he must be about the most tactless man alive, yet at the back of her mind she knew it wasn't his remarks about her appearance that had stung so much. Oh God, it was no use trying to hide it from herself. What had hurt the most was that he hadn't taken her in his arms—hadn't wanted to. Whereas she, in spite of all she'd told herself, *had* wanted it, terribly. Why, she didn't dare to think. And it was all so wrong—because he belonged to Rebie.

She knew that unless he went back to Warathar, or unless Rebie or *someone* turned up, she'd have to leave. Where she'd go she hadn't yet thought, but she'd have to go somewhere—start again.

It was sundown when finally and reluctantly she rode back home. She felt a curious shock in her heart when having handed over her horse to Fred, she encountered Trelawney in the garden. He was getting a barbecue fire going and he had steaks ready nearby. She stopped in her tracks and stared at him, and somehow it was like seeing him for the first time. He looked so—so immaculate, yet so much himself, in his dark red shirt with the sleeves rolled up, his dark pants. His hair for once was relatively tidy—he'd obviously washed it under the shower, and the spectacular vermilion clouds that swarmed across the sky brushed its tawny sheen with fire.

'I'm sorry I'm back late,' she said breathlessly. 'You— you shouldn't have——'

'Shouldn't have what?' His expression mocked her, and she shrank inwardly as his blue-green gaze took in her usual black attire. She'd found some sunblock cream in Rebie's room this morning, so at least she didn't look like a lobster, but that was little comfort just now.

'You shouldn't have started dinner,' she said, 'I'd have
done it. You—you must have known I'd be back.' She was
frightened by the emotions that had begun to race through
her at the mere sight of him, and she was talking fast to
hide them. 'I'll carry on, I'll—I'll make a salad——'

'Calm down, Daisy. There's not a thing for you to do.
The salad's made—everything's prepared. Why don't you
go in and take a shower and change into something
more——' He didn't finish the sentence. His eyes met hers
and she flushed scarlet, remembering, as no doubt he was
too, how she had shouted at him that she'd never want to
look like a woman for him. Then she turned tail and went
inside.

She showered and shampooed her hair, then got dressed
in clean jeans, that the girls had washed that morning, and
her scoop-necked skivvy. What else was there to wear,
after all?

When she rejoined him he had set up a small table under
the mango trees, and he'd even put out two stemmed
glasses and opened a bottle of red wine. As well, he'd lit
a small lamp that seemed to keep the mosquitoes at bay,
even though it attracted the moths quite fatally. What were
they celebrating? she wondered, but didn't dare to ask it
even jokingly. There was just no telling how he'd answer
a question like that.

'Sit down, Daisy,' he told her after giving her one
sweeping sardonic glance. 'This is my party. Just tell me
how you like you steak cooked—well done or *à point*?'

'*A point*,' she said faintly, and couldn't repress a faint
smile. She'd heard Andrew use that phrase often enough,
but somehow she hadn't expected it from Trelawney, which
was probably quite absurd.

'Something's amusing you,' he said coldly. 'Surely you

weren't expecting me to serve you burning steak on the blade of a shovel ... I'll pour you some wine to drink while you're waiting for your steak.' He reached for the bottle and deftly poured her glass to two thirds. Dale murmured her thanks and sipped the wine. He was treating her like a woman, she thought, and she knew he'd really expected her to appear in something feminine. If he only knew, it wasn't possible unless she borrowed some of Rebie's clothes, and she didn't like the idea of doing that. Wearing Rebie's clothes to please the eye of Rebie's fiancé. No—it would never do.

'Where have you been all day?' he asked presently, when the steaks had been served and they'd both helped themselves to green salad.

'I went out for a ride. I knew you wouldn't be interested.'

'In what?' he mocked.

'In—in joining me. Because—well, you won't be able to ride for a while, will you?'

'Not the way I like to ride,' he agreed, and they ate in silence for a few minutes before he remarked, 'I rather thought you might have got into that outfit you were looking at the other night.'

'Did you?' she said without expression, and didn't offer to explain why she hadn't. There were probably two reasons—one was that the clothes weren't hers, and the other was that she wasn't going to back down over what she'd said in the small hours of the morning. Possibly he was trying to make her eat her words. Well, he could try till he was blue in the face, she swore silently. She wouldn't get dressed as a woman for him! It was too dangerous. And so were thoughts like that, and she swerved aside mentally and forced herself to talk to him about some pelicans she'd seen that afternoon.

They had fruit and coffee after the main course, then Dale carried the dishes into the kitchen and stacked them ready for the girls to wash in the morning. Returning outside, she glanced covertly at her watch. It was unnerving to think of spending another couple of hours with Trelawney. So far, he'd said nothing about last night, but she knew he would, eventually, if he had a chance. So instead of sitting down under the mango trees, she told him, 'I'm going for a walk.'

'Good idea,' he said laconically. 'I was going to suggest it myself.'

Dale swallowed. 'On my own,' she said bluntly.

His lip curled. 'Good God, Daisy, not again! I thought I'd talked that nonsense out of you last night.'

'What nonsense?' she asked coldly.

'Brooding—yearning—thinking back to what might have been, or whatever it is you do when you're alone. It doesn't do any good, you know, it only appears to make you touchier than ever. Biting my head off last night when I opened your door.'

'Because you had no right to open it,' she retorted.

'Then you should have let me know you were awake. What the hell were you doing, anyway? Surely not dressing up and reliving the past.'

She turned away and he reached out and took her arm. 'Come on, we'll take that walk,' he said, his voice hard.

'I've changed my mind,' she said instantly. 'I don't want to go for a walk.'

'Okay. Then we'll sit down again.'

She shook her head wildly. 'I'm going inside. The—the moths are driving me crazy.'

'So that's what it is,' he said sarcastically. 'I can put the lamp out.'

'Do whatever you like.' Dale turned her back on him and

marched inside. Once there, she stood uncertainly in the middle of the living room. It was all very well to come inside, but what did she do now? She decided to listen to the radio, and having found some music, she sat down in one of the cane armchairs and reached for a magazine.

As she turned the pages, she saw nothing. Nor did she hear the music. She was thinking about Trelawney, listening for him, wondering if he'd come inside. But of course it was much pleasanter outside, and in fact, she felt very much tempted to go back there herself. But the wine she had drunk had made her sleepy, and she sat on in the warm room, unable to bring herself to make the effort to move. The magazine fell from her hands, and she leaned back in the chair, her eyes closing.

She must have been at least half asleep when with a start she sat up, her eyes wide open. Trelawney had come into the room and was sitting down opposite her.

'Did I startle you?'

'A little. I was listening to the music,' she lied.

'You like Mozart, do you?'

'Very much.'

He smiled slightly. 'You look as if you've been dreaming.'

Dale felt foolish. But it was Mozart, so he was teasing. He leaned back, listening to the music, and Dale followed suit. But she wasn't really listening. She was watching Trelawney, her eyes half closed. He looked so unaware of her, and the longer she looked at him, the more she wanted to have him look back at her. Just to look at her, that was all. There was surely no harm in that. Just to have him acknowledge that she was there.

Then he moved his head slightly, and suddenly their eyes were locked. A jet of flame seemed to shoot through her. She knew it was wrong, but now—now she wanted him to

do more than look at her. She wanted him to cross the
room, to touch her, to put his lips to hers. She couldn't
take her eyes from his, and the strength of her emotions
made her burn with shame. She was absolutely sick with
this terrible longing. Her lips parted—she felt them go soft,
as if at the warmth of a kiss. Her tongue touched her upper
lip, she glanced down at her hands, loosely clasped across
her thigh, and then looked up again. He hadn't moved, and
at the expression in his eyes she tingled all through—felt
the thrilling rising of her blood, felt her limbs go weak.
Trelawney—Trelawney, she thought passionately.

'Daisy.'

He'd said her name aloud, and as he got to his feet she
rose too as though she were in a dream. They moved towards each other across the softly lit room.

It wasn't until the moment when his arms closed around
her that she became conscious of what she'd been doing.
Inviting him—using those tricks she'd learned from Sally.
The parted lips, the slow seductive glances. Oh God, she
shouldn't have. But it was too late now, much too late. He
was crushing her passionately, possessively against him
while his mouth devoured hers, forcing her lips apart so
that his kiss was deep and exciting, making her let go of
everything except the fact that her body was intimately
close to his, and that she was aching for him. His hand
came inside her shirt to find her breast, and she felt his
fingers against her nipples as she clung to him swooningly.

It was Trelawney who broke it up, putting her away
from him and looking down into her face to ask with shat-
tering realism, 'I hope I'm not getting the message wrong,
Daisy—you *are* trying to seduce me, aren't you?'

Dale gasped with shock. How dared he make such an
outrageous accusation? But before she could even begin
to deny it, he went on, 'At all events, lay off, will you?

These damned ribs of mine are giving me hell.'

He was looking down at her and she stared up into his eyes and found she had to swallow down her protests before she could voice them. Because she couldn't blame it all on him this time. He hadn't dragged her out of the chair and into his arms. In fact, she wasn't altogether sure that she hadn't moved first. Still, it hadn't all been her fault, and it was low-minded of him to imply that it was. After all, he needn't have kissed her—not in the way he had—unless he was punishing her for that remark she'd made about his measly little kisses.

She moved a step away from him, her head down. She wanted to cry and she wanted to hide, and she sought wildly in her mind for some way to explain her behaviour —or at least for a way to give back as good as she'd received. She came up with a casually flung, 'I'll lay off gladly! But you're quite wrong—I wasn't trying to seduce you. I—I thought I'd be quite safe—a girl who looks——'

'Butch? Not with that neckline,' he broke in, his eyes on her bosom. 'Not with the look you had on your face when you invited me to do what I did.' He took a few restless steps across the room, then came back to seize her roughly by the wrist.

'Oh hell, Daisy,' he exclaimed. 'You've asked for it— and you're going to get it, and to the devil with my ribs!'

She felt the blood go from her face as she tried to twist out of his grasp. *'Don't!'* she said, her voice husky with alarm.

'Why not?' he said recklessly, his eyes glittering and hard and frightening. 'For my part, I can stand a little pain for a lot of pleasure. And you want it, don't you? Admit it——'

'I don't,' she said violently, but her words were scarcely audible as he jerked her almost off her feet.

'Come on, Daisy, don't renege. You know what it's all about and you want it as much as I do. I'll see you come to no harm.'

'No—please!' She was almost weeping. 'I'm—I'm not——' she panted, but his lips against hers silenced her as he made it clear he was prepared to waste no more time in talk. The fingers of one of his hands was at the waistband of her jeans, and she twisted desperately away from him to gasp out, 'I don't know what it's all about—I —I've never slept with Andrew or with—with anyone.'

'What?' She'd shocked him into relaxing his hold, and she almost fell as she backed away from him. 'You little fraud,' she heard him mutter. 'Are you telling me the truth?'

'Yes—oh yes,' she all but sobbed. 'Anyhow, it would be —wrong. Think of Rebie——'

Trelawney laughed briefly and without amusement. 'You weren't thinking of Rebie a minute ago.' His eye went over her as she pulled down her shirt agitatedly, and held one hand against her mouth as if to hide what his lips had done. 'I could strangle you for what you've just done, Daisy. You don't deserve to get away with it.'

'What?' she asked, agonised, but she knew very well what she'd done and she didn't want him to tell her. She added desperately, 'I'm *sorry*, Trelawney—I didn't mean to——'

'Oh yes, you did,' he said remorselessly. 'You meant every bit of it, darling. You're a very practised little temptress. Is that how you treated your boy-friend? If it is, then I don't wonder he found someone else. One of these days you're going to get exactly what you're asking for—and you can thank your lucky stars it's not going to be tonight.' He turned away abruptly. 'I'm going to take a walk. You'd better disappear.'

Fists clenched tensely, Dale watched him go. She was trembling all over, and her thoughts and emotions were a nightmare-like mixture. She felt overwhelmingly guilty in every way—even over her treatment of Andrew. No way could she hide from herself that she'd almost deliberately inflamed Trelawney just now, and completely lost her own head as well. Standing where he'd left her, she was disturbingly aware of the tumult in her body. She'd never felt this way before—a mass of emotions and ragged nerves and frustration.

She put a hand to her breast and her hammering heart and thought of Rebie and hated herself anew for her disloyalty. But for Rebie, she didn't doubt she'd have allowed Trelawney to go on—to make love to her, and deep in her heart she knew why, though it wasn't something she was ready to face.

As for him—he'd have taken her, but not because he had any tender feelings for her. Simply because she'd aroused him sexually, and because he believed she'd done it before —with Andrew. That was another damning thing. It was entirely her own fault he'd believed she wasn't a virgin. And she hadn't corrected him because she'd wanted to appear fully adult in his eyes—to wipe out the impression she was just 'little Daisy Driscoll'. Had she, even then, had feelings about him that she oughtn't to have?

She turned from her thoughts with repugnance. She hated herself—absolutely hated herself—and she wished she were a thousand miles from here.

CHAPTER SIX

WHEN Trelawney came back from his walk a long time later, Dale had done a lot of thinking and reached the only possible conclusion.

The best place for her *was* a thousand miles away—in Brisbane, with Olivia and her father. Not that she really wanted to go there, but where else was there, at a minute's notice? At least it would be a starting place, and for sure Olivia would see that she was kept busy with the children while she was looking for another job. She couldn't stay here waiting for Rebie forever, anyhow—that was certain. She had to go, and she would tell him tonight, get it over. She'd leave in the morning.

His eyebrows rose as he came into the house and saw her still there, leaning back in the chair. There was anger in his eyes and she wondered uncomfortably if he thought she was looking for more trouble.

'I thought I told you to disappear—to go up to bed,' he said, his nostrils flaring.

Dale got to her feet, feeling slightly sick in the stomach. 'I couldn't—I wouldn't have slept.'

He smiled sardonically, the scar in his cheek deepening. 'I won't ask you why not,' he said, and his greenish gaze ran over her figure, lingering on the scoop neck of her skivvy. 'Or is it just your conscience that's bothering you?'

The colour flared briefly in her cheeks. 'If it is, it's not on your behalf—it's on Rebie's. I've been thinking about things, if you want to know. And I'm leaving—in the morning, early. I thought I should let you know.'

'Good God! What's all this in aid of? Why should you leave?'

Dale's eyes widened. Surely he knew! 'We can't stay here alone.'

'You think not? Well, it's a rather revealing admission on your part. Still, there's no need for melodrama ... As it happens, I've been thinking too—and you're definitely not leaving, so get that into your head.'

'But I must!' she exclaimed. 'I'll—I'll go to Brisbane——'

'You'll do no such thing, Daisy, so shut up and listen to me. Rebie and Kevin know you've turned up here, and God knows what they'll imagine if you disappear in such a hurry. Have you thought of that?' She hadn't, and she murmured something confused before he continued. 'You don't like being here alone with me, so okay. We'll give it another day or two at the most, and if help hasn't come by then, we'll go to Warathar. As you know, I'm doing up the homestead there—I don't intend to live for ever among the remnants of Stephanie's régime. You can set to and start on some chair covers. How about it?'

It was a crazy idea, and Dale said at once, 'I'm not interested in doing sewing for you.'

He shrugged. 'Think of yourself as doing it for Rebie, then. She doesn't like sewing. I'll pay you for it if that will make you feel better. You can look on it as a temporary job. Well?'

Dale, who had recovered from her first reaction, bit her lip. She didn't particularly like his way of putting things, but she didn't really want to go to Brisbane, and she should see Rebie and Kevin. It was what she'd come for, and of course Trelawney was right. It would look very odd if she left now.

She said slowly, 'Well—all right, I suppose I'll do it.

But only to help Rebie, not as a job—for you. And—and on condition we leave here tomorrow.'

'Oh no,' he said at once. 'I'm the one who's making the conditions, Daisy, not you. Don't get the idea I'm begging you to stay. It's all for your benefit. You're not in a bargaining position by any means. We'll give it two more days, that's a decent interval. Surely you can behave yourself for two days,' he finished cynically.

Dale was almost speechless with mortification. And it was pointless to express indignation, because no amount of wishful thinking could alter the way she'd acted earlier in the evening. The less said the better, in fact.

'*I* can,' she said. 'But——'

'You don't trust me? I'm afraid you'll have to. I assure you I shan't invite you to go to bed with me. I'm not really a seducer of virgins ... Well, now that's settled, I'm going up to bed. Goodnight.'

'Goodnight,' she answered almost inaudibly, and as he vanished up the stairs, she threw herself exhaustedly into the armchair. She was a fool to have agreed to stay. And of course he was going to make use of her. He could be as cold and deliberate as that. But she could still change her mind. She could get up early in the morning and drive away and be damned to him. And then heaven knew what Rebie would suspect. She'd have to stay, and she knew it. But—two whole days! Unless Rebie came in the meantime.

Not unexpectedly, Rebie didn't come, and the two days passed almost without mishap. She and Trelawney kept out of each other's way so skilfully that they met only at dinner at night. Dale made more bread the first morning and then went out riding, taking a picnic lunch with her. She knew she'd have to put up with his company for at

least a while after dinner that night, if she didn't want him
to get the idea she couldn't trust herself to behave, so after
coffee she stayed on outside with him. He talked quite
easily and naturally about the stars, and told some story of
getting lost in the bush when he was a child and finding his
way by the Southern Cross. Then he went on to reminisce
about the time he'd spent in Spain—about bulls and bull-
fighting, and the possibility of regarding the latter as a
symbolic and dramatic art form. Dale found herself deeply
interested in his exposition, and she was vastly reassured
by the harmless way the hours passed by.

All the same, she disappeared again the next day, and
after dinner that night chose to stay inside and play some
of Kevin's cassette tapes.

She was considering putting the tapes away when Trelawney remarked, 'Well, tomorrow's the day. It looks like
we head for Warathar.'

'And the sewing machine,' Dale put in, trying for a light
note.

'That's right. And the sewing machine.' His eyes roamed
over her in her usual black gear, and he drawled thoughtfully, 'You know, Daisy, I find it almost unbelievable that
doing the work you do—or used to do—you haven't made
yourself some nice clothes.'

'But I have,' she said.

His eyebrows peaked. 'Then why don't you wear them?
That long skirt and lacy thing you had on the floor the
other night——'

Dale frowned. Didn't he even recognise Rebie's clothes
when he saw them? 'They aren't my things,' she said.
'They were in the wardrobe—I thought they were Rebie's.'

'Maybe they are,' he said, looking sardonically amused.
'I'm not all that familiar with her wardrobe.'

Dale stood up and yawned, and said she was going to bed.

'Our last night alone,' he said. 'You're relieved, are you? Tomorrow we'll have Arnoldine to chaperone us.'

'We hardly need chaperoning,' she said coldly, though her heart had begun to race.

'No? I thought we could have done with it the other night.'

She swallowed, her throat dry. 'Can't we forget that?'

'Can you?' he challenged. 'Personally, I find it difficult —and that's putting it mildly. I wonder continually what makes you tick—and whether you're woman or child.'

'Where you're concerned, it doesn't matter either way,' she said, her voice low. 'Anyway, I don't want to talk about it.'

'You never do, do you?' he said. 'But I rather think you caught yourself out in something the other night, darling.'

'I haven't the least idea what you're talking about,' she said furiously. 'And I wish you wouldn't call me darling. I'm—I'm going up to bed.'

'So am I,' he said, getting up lazily.

Dale knew he was right behind her as she made her way to the stairs. And half way up, in her agitation, she tripped. Trelawney caught hold of her round the waist to stop her from falling, and as she straightened up, she felt his lips brush against her ear.

'Was that deliberate?' he asked, and in the same instant one of his hands moved swiftly up under her shirt to push aside her flimsy bra and find her breast. Desire rose in her instantly and shamefully. Her heart pounded and she could hardly breath. Oh God, she must be mad to feel this way! Trelawney felt nothing for her—it was Rebie whom he loved. But he was a sexy man, and she was there—he'd have behaved this way with any girl——

For the fraction of an instant she let him pull her back
against him, and she closed her eyes and felt his hand
burning against her breast—her nipple hardening in re-
sponse. Then she struggled to free herself.

'Let me go—please.' Her voice broke slightly.

'I don't know that I want to,' he muttered, and in a
panic she tore herself out of his grasp and heard his grunt
of pain as her elbow struck him hard in the chest. She
swung round appalled. Trelawney was leaning back against
the stair rail, one arm across his chest, his face grey, his
eyes closed.

'Trelawney, I'm sorry—are you all right?'

He opened his eyes and they were green and hard and
ruthless.

'I'm perfectly all right. I'm only getting what I asked for.
I should have known better than to expect anything else. I
discovered only the other night what kind of a girl you are,
little Daisy Driscoll.'

'What kind of a girl am I?' she asked, a shiver running
down her spine.

'Ah, so pure,' he said with savage mockery. 'Go on, get up
to your room—get to bed.'

'But you're—hurt,' she protested, agonised. 'I can't just
leave you.'

'For God's sake, what do you think there is to do? I've
told you I'm all right. Now run away—leave me alone ...
Do what I say,' he added with fury as she stood indeter-
minate. 'I don't want you around. Can't you understand
that?'

After a moment she turned from him with a mixture of
hurt and anger. She had awful visions of having driven
the end of his rib into his lungs or something like that, but
of course she hadn't. It would be a good thing when they
were at Warathar, she thought, as she went into her room,

shut the door behind her and leaned against it, waiting for her heart to slow down to normal. Arnoldine—Mrs Miller —they were there and he'd let *them* help him, she was sure, even if he wouldn't let her. She was suddenly conscious that she was rubbing her elbow. It felt jarred, and that told her how hard she had struck him.

Well, he wouldn't let her go. She put her fingers to her mouth, remembering the feel of his hand against her bare flesh. He'd had no right to touch her like that. A man like Trelawney would know exactly what effect it was likely to have—on both of them. So he was right. He'd deserved what he got. He should be more loyal to Rebie, and she was a fool to feel sorry for him.

She heard him moving along the verandah presently, and knew he'd gone to his room. She thought of him there, painfully undressing, and she longed to go and help him—comfort him. Even if he had got no more than he deserved, she still wanted to go and put her arms around him and——

With a sudden fierce movement she crossed the room and turned down the bedclothes. One would almost think she was in love with him. And she wasn't, of course. He was going to marry Rebie.

And that, she knew deep in her heart, was the only thing that was stopping her ...

They left for Warathar the next day in Dale's car. Neither of them mentioned his injured ribs, and Dale had the idea it had hurt his pride that a mere girl could have made him gasp with pain as he had. She felt dreadful about it, despite herself—guilty and helpless. But at least he let her do the driving, and that gave her something else to think about.

He had told Fred they were going, and Dale had made

sure when Lila and Susie came that everything in the house was left spick and span. She'd left a slightly garrulous note for Rebie, trying to give the impression she felt as remote from Trelawney as she had been as a child. 'I know you don't like sewing, so I've prevailed on him to let me start it for you. It's rather dreary here with no one else around, and I think his chest is pretty painful, though he never says a thing about it. It will be better for him at Warathar with other women around to look after him. He thinks I'm still twelve years old, so I can't do a thing. See you soon! Daisy.'

It was some fifty kilometres to the home station, and they were long slow kilometres through that rugged country, even in a car. There was one river crossing to make, but there was the merest trickle of water moving down the middle of the sandy bed, though Dale knew that in the Wet the creek could turn into a roaring torrent in a matter of hours.

She'd been to Warathar only once before and her memories of it were vague. There were the usual outbuildings—men's quarters, a meat house, machinery shed and so on, and she pulled up outside the garden as Trelawney instructed her to do. He carried the bags in spite of his ribs, and she went ahead of him into the garden, leafy and pleasant with its peperinas, red-flowered oleanders, and tall bamboos. At one side was a red ant-bed tennis court, which she remembered, at the other side a swimming pool, edged with blue tiles, and with a fantastic row of tall date palms near by, casting their reflections on the still water.

Dale exclaimed involuntarily, 'Oh, I remember those palms! But the pool's new, isn't it?'

'Fairly new. Ray had it put in for Stephanie a few years ago. Coming from the coast, she's keen on swimming

You're partial to the water too, aren't you?'

'Yes. But I only have my bikini,' she said, giving him a sideways glance. 'And you don't approve of that, do you?'

'Oh, there'll be no one around for a while. And I shan't be bothering you,' he said sardonically.

Point taken, thought Dale, feeling slightly rebuffed.

The homestead, L-shaped and single-storied, was older than the house at Jackalass, older and very solid and very well kept. Its timbers were painted off-white, its iron roof was green, and so were the new-looking awnings that shaded the wide verandah. Built well up on the high side of the river above the waterhole, it had never yet been flooded, and possibly never would be. As they drew near a woman came across the verandah to meet them, and Dale recognised Arnoldine Bell instantly. Trelawney had telephoned her that they were coming, so she was unsurprised, and well prepared.

Dale had wondered if Arnoldine would have changed much and as she went up the two low steps on to the verandah, she saw that she hadn't. She wore a sleeveless chalk white dress that had a slightly shaggy texture, and a neckline so plunging that beside it Dale's scoop-necked skivvy would have looked almost Puritan. Her curves were a little too pronounced for her to be called slim, and her hair was short and black and glossy, curving in a fringe above neatly arched eyebrows. Dale had always thought her pretty, but she was quite beautiful—a woman with a very feminine, slightly mysterious aura about her. It was only from really close up that her age showed. Make-up couldn't conceal the coarsened texture of her tanned skin, the ravages of the cruel outback climate. And her eyes—they were far from young. But then, as Rebie had rather unkindly remarked, she must be going on for forty.

She greeted Trelawney before she turned to Dale to exclaim, 'Well, Dale, this is a surprise! You haven't changed a great deal, have you? You're thin and anxious looking as ever. Come along inside out of the heat. I've put her in the end bedroom,' she said to Trelawney over her shoulder.

She hadn't asked him about his accident, Dale noted, and wondered if she even knew about it yet. Well, she'd keep quiet until she discovered how much Arnie knew. She wasn't going to be accused of telling tales about anything whatsoever, she was going to be very discreet.

She followed Arnoldine into the house, reflecting that there was nothing of the governess about her now. In fact, from her attitude, one would have guessed her to be the mistress of the house ... Trelawney deposited Dale's suitcase on the bed in the end bedroom before he disappeared, and Arnoldine perched herself gracefully on the arm of a chair and told Dale, 'Get your unpacking done right away, Dale. It's a cold lunch and it can wait half an hour. You don't want your clothes to be crushed.'

Dale fiddled with the catch of her suitcase. Old habits, it seemed, died hard, and even though Arnie no longer looked like a governess, it was still second nature for Dale to do as she told her. But in this case it was ridiculous, her clothes being what they were.

After a second she said awkwardly, 'I haven't brought anything that matters, Arnoldine. Only jeans and shorts and shirts. I can unpack later.' She opened her suitcase reluctantly and took out her toilet things, then crossed to the dressing table. Her reflection was the opposite of reassuring. She looked gauche, coltish, a complete contrast to the very poised Arnoldine who at that moment was leaning forward to adjust the strap of her white sandal. The low neckline was very obvious, and Dale thought involuntarily, 'She must sunbathe in the nude to be tanned as far down as that.' By the beautiful blue-tiled pool, of course. There was no need these days for her to go out along the creek to one of those places where Dale and the Vining children used to dive and splash and scream in what seemed another age. She had it really good at Warathar.

Dale brushed her too short hair away from her ears, and hated the sight of herself in her old jeans and vest. In the mirror, she saw Arnoldine straighten up before asking her, 'And what are you doing with yourself these days, Dale?'

Dale gave a slight start of guilt and turned her back on the mirror. But of course Arnie wasn't asking what she'd been doing at *Jackalass*—and she said hastily, 'Oh, nothing terribly exciting. I don't live with my father now. When he—they—moved to Brisbane, I decided to make the break, and I didn't go with them.'

'That sounds sensible.' Arnoldine crossed one bare brown leg over the other. 'Your stepmother was obviously reluctant to have you, wasn't she? How many children are there now?'

'Three,' said Dale. 'Stuart and Kim and little Jonathan.'

'Quite a family,' Arnoldine commented. 'We realised you'd moved, of course. When Beth died we thought of you, but the last letter we'd sent you had been returned.'

Dale bit her lip. 'I should have written long ago——'

'Oh well, one can't maintain contact for ever, and after all, we've seen nothing at all of you since you left.'

'No. Well, I couldn't come during the holidays—Olivia's health wasn't good while the children were little and I had to help.'

'Oh dear, does that sound like a sob story?' Arnoldine said with faint mockery.

'If it does, I didn't mean it that way,' said Dale, a little annoyed. 'Anyhow, I went to Rockhampton soon after my family moved. I was offered a job there with a decorating firm, I did the soft furnishings.'

'Really! Then what's brought you out here to us? Holidays?'

To *us*? Dale thought. But after all, Arnoldine had lived out here for years. Ashamed of what was undoubtedly a twinge of jealousy, she said quickly, 'No, not holidays. My job didn't work out as well as I'd expected. I've given it up, and I'm not working just now.'

Arnoldine's black eyes looked scathing. 'Surely you're not one of these girls who don't stick at a job because it isn't—fulfilling or something of the sort. You used to be quite a dependable child.'

Dale discovered she didn't like being taken to task, but she had no intention of confiding her personal problems in Arnoldine, so she merely said quietly, 'I liked my work. I'll find another job when I go back.'

'And when will that be?' Arnoldine asked sweetly, and waited for an answer, but Dale didn't see that she had very much right to be questioning her going and comings.

'I haven't a clue,' she said with a shrug.

Arnoldine smiled slightly, quite unperturbed. 'You think it's none of my business, don't you? But I'm the housekeeper here, Dale, and what you do does concern me. You've arrived without any warning, and I think I have some right to know how long you intend to stay.'

Dale bit her lip. 'I'm sorry, Arnie——'

'Arnoldine, please. You know I dislike diminutives.'

'Sorry,' Dale said again, and amended her previous impression. There was plenty of the governess left after all. 'I was going to say—how long I stay really depends on Rebie—Rebecca.'

Arnoldine's eyebrows went up and her darkly lashed eyes widened. 'For goodness' sake, why? This is not Rebecca's home.'

'No, but it will be when she and Trelawney are married,

won't it?' said Dale. 'That's one reason why I'm here, actually—at Warathar, I mean. I'm going to get the new furnishings started.'

'That's ridiculous!' Arnoldine said sharply. 'How this homestead is decorated is nothing at all to do with you—a mere dropper in. If Rebecca wants things altered, then she must see to it herself. I'm surprised she isn't here with you today, as a matter of fact.'

'She's out at the muster,' Dale explained, sitting on the edge of the bed. 'She has to help entertain the guests.'

'Has to? What nonsense!' Arnie looked hard at Dale, who reflected absently, 'It's her eyes that stop her from looking really young.' They were such knowing eyes, so worldly wise. The thought disturbed her because it made her think of Trelawney—and the sleepwalking incident. Somehow, more than ever, she felt she must stick up for Rebie.

'It isn't nonsense,' she protested. 'Philippa wouldn't like to stay at the camp unless Rebie was there too. One girl couldn't stay on her own with all those men.'

Arnoldine wasn't in the least impressed. 'Really, Dale, does Philippa have to stay at the camp? I can't believe she's much use there. A city girl is more likely to be a nuisance than anything else. It seems to me Rebecca should never have invited guests to come in the first place. There she is, newly engaged, and already she has to divert herself with other people. She thinks of no one but herself.'

Dale looked at her moodily. She did have a down on Rebie, and she wasn't being very just.

'I don't imagine Rebie invited the Richards,' she commented. 'They're Kevin's guests—I had the distinct impression he's serious about Philippa. Naturally she's interested in seeing all she can of the place, and so is Ivor.'

Arnie shook her head and smiled ruefully, and the smile

emphasised how weathered her skin was—but didn't detract from her undoubted charm. 'Dale, you're like a child with your naïve interpretation of the situation! Kevin's only met Philippa two or three times. The fact is, the Richards are Rebecca's guests. They're friends of hers from Brisbane. She may be engaged to Trelawney, but she's bored at Jackalass, and always has been. As for Ivor, I don't really think it's the outback he's interested in seeing.'

Dale glanced away from her. Arnie sounded as if she knew what she was talking about, and she remembered uneasily that when she and Trelawney had left the muster camp, Ivor and Rebie were pretty plainly going to spend the rest of the afternoon together. But it hadn't worried Trelawney, and with all his experience, one would think he could recognise a potential rival.

'There's such a thing as a platonic friendship, Arnie,' she said defiantly.

'Who said there wasn't?' the other woman retorted, her dark eyes maliciously mocking. 'And please don't shorten my name, Dale. Now if you aren't going to change, we may as well go and have some lunch.'

With an inward sigh, Dale followed her from the room. It occurred to her that there were more complications in this situation than she'd imagined. And she herself was a great deal more involved than she liked . . .

Rather unwillingly that afternoon, she allowed Trelawney to take her out to the station store to see the furnishing fabrics that were available for redecorating.

'You might like to start with the sitting room,' he suggested as she stood in the big room with its piles of tinned foods, bags of sugar and flour, saddles, boots, and practically everything one could imagine. 'We need new curtains, and the sofa and chairs could do with new loose covers. Are you capable of making those?'

'Yes,' she said warily, her glance skimming over the bolts of furnishing fabrics stacked up on a shelf next to some dress materials. She noted with approval that they were all cottons and synthetics, which meant they'd stand up well to the frequent laundering made necessary by the dust and heat and humidity of the outback climate. 'If you'll tell me what Rebie's planned——'

'Good heavens, Rebie hasn't had time to give it a thought yet,' he said with a lift of his eyebrows. 'You'll have to rely on your own good taste and know-how.'

Dale shot him a quick look and was disconcerted to find his greenish eyes on her, a look of amusement in them. She ran her fingers nervously through her short hair, and moved away to finger a bolt of fine-textured cotton in muted green. It would hang beautifully, and it would look just right in the sitting room, replacing the pretentious gold brocade curtains she'd noticed there after lunch. And the cotton chintz next to it—that would be just right for loose covers, and it was a perfect match. But all the same, it was for Rebie to decide.

'Well?' said Trelawney with masculine abruptness, and she said coolly,

'I'd rather you and Rebie made the decisions. It's nothing to do with me.'

His eyebrows rose sardonically. 'I thought I was consulting a professional.' He moved to stand beside her. 'I had this lot sent out from Townsville before anything had happened between Rebie and me, of course. So if you're afraid of taking the responsibility, you needn't be. It will all be on my head.' He turned towards her and his arm brushed against hers and she drew away quickly. 'How about the green for the curtains?'

'All right,' she agreed. 'But I won't do anything else—not till Rebie comes.'

Till Rebie comes! It seemed to Dale she had done nothing but wait for Rebie since she came outback—and now Arnie had been hinting that she was having a flirtation with a friend from Brisbane. If that was so, she might be waiting a good while longer yet.

'I'll get someone to carry that bolt along to the sewing room for you,' Trelawney said brusquely. 'I think you'll find all you want there.'

When they parted, she didn't go straight to the sewing room. She went to the kitchen to renew her acquaintance with Mrs Miller, and once again she was recognised instantly.

'Daisy Driscoll!' the cook exclaimed, and hugged her warmly. 'Arnoldine said you were coming, but I'd have known you anywhere. You haven't changed a scrap. Not like me—I've put on that much weight! Well, it's lovely to see you—I hope you still like orange meringue pie! It used to be your favourite dessert, and I'm planning to have that tonight.'

'That's sweet of you, Mrs Miller. It's still my favourite —but nobody makes it like you used to.'

'Rebie didn't come along with you,' the cook commented, frowning a little.

'No, she can't get away just yet.' Dale played around with the facts a little as she explained, 'Kevin wanted her at Jackalass because of the guests, you see.'

'Yes, I see. It's a shame Trelawney had that accident. He'd have enjoyed the company too. I hope he's been looking after himself.'

'Oh, he has,' said Dale. 'He's got his chest well strapped up.' She coloured faintly remembering what she herself had done to him the other night, and now she was talking as if she were all concern.

'Well, nothing's killed him yet,' the cook said. 'And

broken ribs aren't all that serious, after all. How are you going to pass the time here? Wouldn't you sooner be with the others at Jackalass?'

'Not really,' Dale shrugged. 'I'm going to make curtains for the sitting room, as a matter of fact.' She laughed a little as Mrs Miller's mouth fell open.

'Rebie's palmed that off on you! She's a very naughty girl, then. It's not fair.'

Dale shook her head smilingly. 'I've been sewing professionally for the last two or three years, Mrs Miller. You don't have to feel sorry for me. It won't worry me a bit. And Rebie didn't palm it off on me—I offered to do it,' she concluded, thinking of the note she'd left.

'Well, you're a true friend ... what do you think of the engagement? You were surprised, I'll bet. I'd never have guessed Trelawney would settle for Rebie. Buff now, he always had a soft spot for her, and if he hadn't left Jackalass when he did, I often think something might have come of it. Rebie's too young for him in my view, and not nearly as well suited to outback life. But there—I'm gossiping and I oughtn't ... You make yourself at home here, Daisy, and any time you're hungry come along to the kitchen and have a snack. You could do with a little fattening up.'

Oh dear, Dale thought ruefully as she left the kitchen and headed for the sewing room. Everyone seemed to think she needed fattening up. For no reason at all, she thought of Arnoldine's curvaceous figure, and that made her wonder if there were any one-piece swimsuits in the store. It would be nice to take a swim in the pool, but she felt self-conscious about wearing her bikini. Maybe she'd sink her pride and ask Trelawney about swimsuits some time. And maybe she wouldn't.

Meanwhile in the sewing room, she noted that the bolt of material had already been carried across, and she found a tape measure and went along to the sitting room to start work. That after all was what she was here for.

It should have reminded her of Andrew, and it should have hurt. But it didn't.

CHAPTER SEVEN

DALE worked on the curtains for the next three days. There were a good many of them—floor to ceiling and along two walls. She was pinch-pleating them, and it was going to be a very professional job.

Trelawney took no interest. He didn't ask if she'd started, how she was progressing, or anything at all. He might have been, like Rebie, miles away, and it irked her even while she was telling herself she was glad. She saw him at mealtimes, and that was about all. And at mealtimes Arnoldine did most of the talking. She knew all about his damaged ribs by now, and she'd apparently taken him in hand— ordering him to rest, checking on his strapping and so on. Dale couldn't help observing that he didn't object to *her* attentions and he certainly never told her not to fuss over him. Maybe it was because she was capable and Dale wasn't, or maybe it was for another reason.

Spending most of the day in the sewing room, Dale hadn't much idea what went on in the rest of the house. Except that Mrs Miller brought her morning and afternoon tea and admired her efficiency while she stayed to chat a little, no one took any notice of her. But lateish on the third afternoon, Arnoldine appeared in the sewing room. She'd obviously been in the pool, for her dark hair was damp and over her swimsuit she wore a cotton wrap-around gown that reached half way down her thighs.

'What an industrious girl you've grown to be,' she remarked, an edge of mockery in her voice. She sat down on a chair by the open door that led on to the verandah and looked around the room. 'I should feel gratified, seeing I had quite a hand in your education. Who are you doing all this for, I wonder? Rebecca? Or Trelawney?'

Dale, machining down one side of a long curtain, went steadily on with it, though her heart had given an uncomfortable leap.

'For Rebie, of course,' she said, hoping she sounded unmoved.

'But why of course?' Arnoldine persisted. 'You and Rebecca are hardly close friends after all this time apart. You haven't developed a crush on Trelawney, I hope.'

'No, I haven't,' Dale snapped furiously. Head down, she kept the machine going full tilt.

'I hope you mean it,' said Arnoldine. 'The number of girls who've fallen for him is legion.'

'Well, he's safely engaged now,' Dale pointed out. The bobbin thread ran out and she proceeded to deal with that. She told herself she didn't want to engage in a conversation about Trelawney with Arnoldine. Despite the engagement, Arnie sounded decidedly proprietorial, and it disturbed Dale, though not only on Rebie's behalf.

There was a silence of several seconds before the other woman said, her voice hard, 'That engagement is a farce —an absurdity.' She crossed her legs and arranged the hem of her gown carefully, above knees that were smooth and brown and, Dale had to admit, pretty. 'Of course Rebecca's always fancied herself as a member of the squatocracy, even though David was only manager of the outstation here. I sometimes think she'd convinced herself that old Mr Saber would leave Jackalass to her father, when he died. It's not a case of loving the Gulf country—she doesn't love it, and no one can convince me otherwise. It's the case of being in love with the notion of a prestige background.'

Dale held her tongue for a minute. Arnie was certainly intent on knocking Rebie! Then she glanced up from the machine as the thread spun on, filling the bobbin spool, and said innocently, 'Isn't she lucky Trelawney's asked her to marry him, then? She'll *really* be someone.'

'Lucky!' Arnoldine said scornfully, getting up from her chair. 'The moment she came to housekeep for Kevin she started throwing herself at him. She was *always* at Warathar—and quite uninvited. I only hope he wakes up to himself before it's too late. If not, he'll find himself with an absentee wife most of the year. She'll be over at the coast, showing off to her friends, that's my prediction. She doesn't love our sunburnt country and never has. It's a pity she can't satisfy herself with David's property at Charters Towers. It may be small compared with Warathar, but Trelawney says he's made a good buy, and it will be a very valuable little place.' With that, she drifted from the room, and Dale looked after her thoughtfully. She *was* possessive. *Our* sunburnt country, she'd said. Did she think she belonged here more than Rebie did? Obviously yes—and certainly she seemed to have been a fixture on the property for a good many years. 'If I were Rebie,' Dale thought, 'I'd hate knowing she was here.' Yet what could Rebie do about it? If she were older—as old as Mrs Miller—it would be quite different. As it was, she might be a few years older than Trelawney, but she still looked so vital, so attractive, and that was what made it all so wrong.

Dale felt a mass of nerves, worrying about it on Rebie's account. Or *was* that what she was doing? She wished she'd never agreed to come to Warathar. She really should have gone to Brisbane and left it to Trelawney to deal with

any suspicions Rebie might have. He had claimed it was all
for her benefit, but she couldn't see that. He just liked to
have everything his own way, to twist women round his
little finger, though he didn't seem able to do that with
Rebie. She was going her own way, and perhaps that was
what appealed to him.

But could he possibly be using her, Dale, to bring Rebie
to heel? she wondered. It was so unlikely it was laughable.
Rebie would never be jealous of her, as one glance in the
mirror could convince her at any time. She wasn't, these
days, anything like the devastating girl who had persuaded
Andrew MacWade to fall in love with her.

Suddenly restless, Dale decided she'd do no more sewing. Leaving the bobbin spool still on the spindle, she
stood up and let the curtain she'd been making fall to the
floor. It had been a boiling hot day. In her black jeans she
was stifling, and she thought it mean of Arnie not to have
invited her to join her at the pool—though perhaps she'd
been there with Trelawney.

'Well, who cares?' she asked herself impatiently. She
moved to the door and looked into the garden. Her nostrils
were filled with the scent of wet earth, and she knew that
earlier in the day Arnoldine had watered the long troughs
of green ferns that stood all along the inner wall of the
verandah. She went round to her room, took off her clothes
and got into her bikini. She'd put on a little weight since
she'd been here, she noted absently. That was due to Mrs
Miller's cooking, no doubt.

A few minutes later, she was cooling off in the pool. The
sky was swarming with rapidly crimsoning clouds, and the
tall date palms stood dramatically silhouetted against them.
Floating on her back, she thought, 'I love this sunburnt
country,' and some of the words of Dorothea Mackellar's
poem, that Arnie had made her and the Vining children

learn years ago, drifted through her mind.

'All you who have not loved her, You will not understand,' she said aloud, and unexpectedly her eyes were full of tears. Flipping herself over in the water, she swam rapidly the length of the pool and back.

The colour went from the sky and the light began to fade, and she pulled herself out on to the warm smooth tiles, pressing the water from her hair and thinking that she should have brought a towel from the house.

'Here, take this, Daisy.'

It was Trelawney, and her heart turned over. She swung round and discovered he was holding out a towel for her. She took it and wrapped it quickly round her almost naked body, that looked pale in the fading light.

'Thank you,' she said, tossing back her hair and blinking water from her eyes. She added nervily, 'I hope I'm not in disgrace for swimming in your pool in a bikini. Or is that why you're here with an instant cover-up for me?' she concluded flippantly.

'No, darling,' he said, regarding her mockingly. 'My motives was purely altruistic. I thought you'd want to rub your hair dry.'

'I prefer to—to dry my body,' she said uneasily. 'And now I'm going inside to shower and dress.'

'That could be a pity,' he murmured.

'What do you mean?' she asked, and immediately wished the words back. It wasn't always wise to ask Trelawney what he meant, as she'd discovered often enough before.

'Simply that you're a whole lot more attractive when you're not wearing your usual black get-up,' he said.

'It doesn't matter how I look,' she retorted, unnerved.

'No? You might find it matters when Rebie turns up,' he said. 'I intend asking Kevin and the Richards to Warathar after the muster, too. You'll certainly look very striking coming to dinner in your faded black jeans and your tatty little shirt. I realise you're contra-suggestible, but I'm going to advise you to have a consultation with Arnoldine some time and see if she can come to the rescue with something wearable. She has a rather fuller figure than you have, but no doubt she'll find something that will more or less fit you ... Did you pour out your soul to Rebie about your love affair, by the way?'

'No. And I'm sorry I told *you* anything about it——'

'You didn't have much choice, did you?' he commented. 'I seem to recall I twisted your arm. Well, you needed to talk. Talking eases the pain if you find a sympathetic listener.'

'Which cuts you out,' she retorted.

'Well, it's not really possible for you to cry on my shoulder as things are, is it?'

Dale drew away from him. 'I don't want to talk about that sort of thing.'

'God knows, it's probably one of the topics we should avoid,' he agreed. 'Somehow or other I'm always ending up with you in my arms.'

'I can't think why,' she said, her breath quickening. 'It's not something I want to happen, I assure you.'

'Nor I,' he said dryly. 'I do have a fiancée, however unofficially, and I'm no more fond of disloyalty than you are.'

'I'm relieved to hear it,' she said faintly. 'Now would you please let me pass? I'm going inside.'

'By all means.' He stepped aside and Dale hurried past him. She felt stirred up and frustrated. It was better, she thought, not to see him on her own at all.

Next morning at breakfast, Arnoldine told her she was driving Trelawney to the round up at the Warathar end of the run, and Dale, pouring coffee, spilled some on the tablecloth. Surely they'd ask her to go along too—hadn't she been working like a slave for the past three days? Or weren't they even aware of that? She looked across the table and encountered Trelawney's hare-green eyes.

'You'll want to get on with your curtain making, Daisy,' he said, making it an unarguable fact.

Dale stared at him smoulderingly. She was sick and tired of sewing. She'd far sooner have a day off and go out to the muster with him and Arnoldine. She said tentatively, not wanting to invite herself along and risk a rebuff, 'I've just about finished those curtains.'

'Good,' he said unrelentingly. 'If you get them off your hands today you'll be able to start on the loose covers. You'll find the key of the store in the office. That chintz stuff is what Rebie had in mind. Mrs Miller will help you carry it to the sewing room.'

Dale blinked. *Rebie* had it in mind? But he'd told her Rebie hadn't made any plans. About to exclaim, she desisted. Arnie was looking at her intently, one elbow on the table, as if she were eager to hear Dale's comment. And when Dale said nothing after all, she murmured, 'My goodness, how lucky Rebecca is to have a friend like you, Dale.'

Dale longed to make a face at her, to poke out her tongue childishly, which was strange, because she'd never done that when she was a child. Rebie had, though.

She watched them drive away across the paddock, followed by a little cloud of red dust, and she felt utterly depressed. Arnoldine had insisted on doing the driving. It's better for you to save yourself from *any* exertion,' she'd told Trelawney, and he'd submitted without a murmur. That was funny, Dale thought, because in her experience he was far more inclined to play down the severity of his injury than to play it up.

She didn't go out to the sewing room. She got into her

bikini and went out to the pool. After she'd had a swim she stretched out on a towel in the shade.

At eleven o'clock Mrs Miller brought her some tea and scones. She was longing for the tea, but though the scones looked delicious and would be infinitely light—no one who had tasted Mrs Miller's sour cream scones could ever forget them—she wasn't hungry. There were three scones, oozing with butter, and Mrs Miller told her firmly, 'Now you eat those all up, Daisy—though I do believe you're getting a little more flesh on your bones the last few days. Why didn't you go out to the muster camp with Arnoldine and Trelawney?'

'I thought Rebie might turn up,' Dale lied. 'Besides, I want to get those curtains finished.'

'You mustn't be too conscientious,' the cook reproved her, her hands on her plump hips. 'You haven't come all this way to lock yourself up and work twelve hours a day. You've got to enjoy yourself sometimes, and you shouldn't let Trelawney bully you. The trouble is he has such— what's the word people use nowadays? Charisma—is that what I mean?'

'I suppose so,' Dale said uneasily.

'Yes. So you're leaning over backwards to do what he wants. You just relax a little and enjoy yourself—get Arnoldine to give you a game of tennis some time. *He* can't play with those broken ribs, but he's not so much of an invalid as he make out, you know. Yesterday I saw him go down to the horse paddock while Arnoldine was watering the house plants. He went for a ride too. Well, I must get back to my kitchen. Come in if you want more scones, I made a good big batch.'

'Oh, I won't want any more!' Dale exclaimed, patting her flat stomach, and Mrs Miller laughed.

Later she took her tray to the kitchen, then went into

her bedroom and pulled on a pair of blue denim shorts. Barefooted, and still wearing her bikini bra, she considered what she was going to do next. She positively was not going to finish those curtains today. As for the loose covers, she was quite sure Rebie didn't even know the chintz existed.

Standing in the middle of the room, she thought of that dig Trelawney had made about her having no clothes fit to wear at dinner when the others were here. It was perfectly true, but she didn't want to rely on Arnoldine's coming to the rescue. No—she had a better idea than that.

With sudden decision she went to Trelawney's office and took the key to the stores from its hook on the wall. Then, on her way out, she called in at the kitchen.

'I'm going into the store, Mrs Miller. Trelawney said I might—to get some chintz and—er—a shirt for myself.'

'You could certainly do with another shirt, Daisy,' Mrs Miller agreed with a smile. 'I've been wondering why you always wear those shabby old black things. I'll be glad to see the last of them.'

Her expression invited confidences, but feeling rather mean, Dale didn't explain. She went outside and through the garden to the store, and there she selected two checked shirts for herself, and a pair of beige jeans that fitted her remarkably well. That done, she considered the bolts of dress materials. Stripes, checks, plain cottons—they were more suited to house dresses and shirts than anything else. Then, among the furnishing fabrics, something caught her eye. Right at the back of the shelf was a very nearly empty bolt of soft silky brocade. She hadn't seen anything like it around the house, but it had probably been used for curtains years ago, when Stephanie was first here perhaps, or even longer ago than that. Deep mossy green with a delicate pattern of golden ferns. In a few seconds she'd reached it down and ascertained that there'd be enough for a dress.

Only just. Ankle-length, sleeveless, straight—it would need a split skirt. Excitedly she folded it up and draped it over her arm, loving the cool soft feel of it. It was a gorgeous shade and would enhance the colour of her eyes, while the ferns were an almost exact match for her hair, which by now had reached the stage where a little of its wave was starting to reappear.

She carried her trophies to her room before she asked Mrs Miller to help her with the chintz, and after that she had lunch.

By late afternoon she'd finished making her dress except for some hand finishing. She hung it away in her wardrobe, and decided to say nothing about it to Trelawney or Arnoldine. They came home at sundown, looking, she couldn't help thinking as she watched them cross the garden together, like a married couple. So established—so used to each other. She tried to picture Rebie at Trelawney's side, but she couldn't. Arnoldine looked so right. And of course she would be right—she was so capable, so decorative. In fact she had everything. Yet he hadn't asked her to marry him. He'd asked Rebie ...

That night there was the first of the electric storms that always came before the beginning of the Wet. Far out across the paddocks lightning danced and flickered, illuminating the great clouds that had gathered on the horizon. There was a faintly unpleasant scent in the air which Dale recognised with a shock of remembrance as the smell of the gidgee. It always smelt like that when the Wet was on its way. Rain must have fallen somewhere on the property, and Dale had a feeling of restlessness and urgency, as if something must happen, and happen soon.

She and Trelawney and Arnoldine sat on the verandah watching the lightning display and talking very little. Trelawney smoked, which he rarely did, and Dale thought he looked moody. She was wondering if it was because of Rebie's non-appearance—or even if he was regretting his engagement. Goodness knew what Arnoldine might have been saying to him during the day they had spent together. In a way she didn't blame Arnoldine for not wanting Rebie and Trelawney to marry. It would certainly mean the end of her time here, and what on earth would she do then? Where would she go? Dale felt a decided twinge of pity for her.

She came out of her reverie as Trelawney stood up and said abruptly, 'If you'll excuse me, I'm going to bed.'

'You've had a tough day,' said Arnoldine, looking up at him and smiling gently. 'Take a shower, why don't you —and then let me come and make sure you get that rib belt on really comfortably.'

'Give me half an hour,' he said. Then with an almost curt 'Goodnight, Daisy,' he went inside.

A moment later, without an excuse, Arnoldine went inside too.

Dale, sitting on alone, felt herself burn with a feeling that she soon recognised with shame as jealousy. How crazy could you get? She wished she'd never caught up with Trelawney Saber again.

Another day passed, and the mail came—and it was Arnoldine who drove Trelawney out to the station airstrip to receive it when the Cessna came down. In an effort to occupy her mind, Dale went to the sewing room to finish the curtains. She heard the others come back and knew that Trelawney would be in the office sorting the mail. She hadn't written any letters and didn't expect to receive any. Alone in the sewing room, she began measuring up the chair covers.

Late in the afternoon of the next day the stockmen began

arriving back at the homestead with the mob of sale
cattle. Dale, in the sewing room and perspiring in the heat,
heard them come and went on to the verandah. The yards
near the homestead were full of bellowing beasts, the air
was thick with dust, the place swarmed with men and
horses. She stood and watched, and her heart lifted as she
caught some of the feeling of excitement she remembered
from summers long ago at Jackalass. The station had come
alive, the feeling of isolation, of being cut off from the
world, had somehow gone. It was as though a page had
turned, a new chapter of life begun.

That night there was a fourth person at the dinner table
—Murray Hewson, Trelawney's jackeroo, a rather quiet
serious man in his late twenties. The talk at dinner was
all of cattle, and while Arnoldine leaned forward, her face
animated, joining in the conversation, Dale sat silent. She
suspected the jackeroo didn't quite know what to make of
her, but she didn't care terribly about that. What hurt, and
was beginning to hurt more and more, was that Trelawney
had more or less ignored her for days.

Later, on the verandah, they watched what had become
a nightly display of lightning. The other three drank beer,
Dale had a glass of lemonade, and at last the subject of
cattle was dropped and the talk turned to personalities.

'What's the news from Buff?' Trelawney asked Murray.
'I noticed you had a letter from her. Is she coming back
soon?'

'She doesn't say so,' the jackeroo said. 'I reckon she
doesn't like leaving her father on his own.'

'Try and talk some sense into her,' Trelawney said
briefly, then turned to Dale. 'By the way, Daisy, Rebie
will be here tomorrow. Kevin says he can't get away just
yet, but I daresay the Richards will be along.'

'I doubt it,' said Arnoldine, her dark eyes sparkling.

'Dale tells me Kevin's fallen in love with Philippa. He probably won't want to let her out of his sight.'

'Is that a fact?' Trelawney frowned down at his glass. 'Well, Rebie won't come on her own, you can be sure of that. She's no intrepid outback explorer—she continually has visions of losing herself between one paddock and the next.'

'Ivor will hardly be much help,' Arnoldine commented sweetly. 'A city man——'

'Rebie knows the way well enough,' Trelawney said irritably. 'All she needs is a little moral support.'

'From Ivor? Oh.' Arnoldine smiled, suppressed it quickly, and finished her drink. She managed to suggest, to Dale's ears at least, that moral support was the last kind of service Ivor was likely to provide . . .

When Dale got up next morning she put on the beige pants and one of the checked shirts she'd taken from the stores. Then she brushed her hair hard and looked at herself critically in the mirror. She looked good. She could imagine the approval in Trelawney's eyes as he looked at her, and she glowed a little. Then she turned away from the mirror, unbuttoned the shirt and took it off, unzipped the jeans and changed into her usual black ones. That sort of thing was not to be encouraged—dressing up for Trelawney. Her mouth set as she pulled on her black vest.

Trelawney looked at her hard when she came out to the breakfast table. He rose from his chair and watched her cross the room, his lip curling, a cynical expression in his greenish eyes. Dale felt exactly as if he knew she'd put on other clothes, then changed out of them. But he couldn't. And he could only know about the shirt if Mrs Miller had told him.

As she sat down to her breakfast, he commented, 'I hope you haven't forgotten we have visitors coming today.'

'No, I haven't forgotten,' she said, aware that Arnie was listening intently. The jackaroo had gone off to work hours ago. 'When will they be here?'

'I couldn't say ... How are the furnishings progressing?'

Dale shrugged. He hadn't taken much interest before; now, because Rebie was arriving, he wanted to know.

'You got the chintz?'

'Yes,' she said uncommunicatively.

'Well,' he pressed her, 'how *are* you progressing?'

Arnoldine raised her head. 'Don't embarrass the child, Trelawney. Loose covers are not the easiest things in the world to make. They need quite a degree of skill and perseverance. I know, because I made some at Jackalass for Beth. You mustn't expect *too* much of Dale.'

Dale bristled. She had plenty of skill and she wasn't lacking in perseverance. She was quite positive that if it came to the point she could make a set of covers far more professional than anything Arnie could produce—and in half the time as well. She had her own reasons for not racing ahead, and she told Arnoldine blandly, 'I'm not embarrassed in the least, Arnie. I should think I'm a lot more capable than you are when it comes to making loose covers—or curtains either, for the matter of that. I can practically do them blindfold, if you'd like to know.'

Arnoldine stiffened and Dale almost giggled, she looked so governessy.

'Please don't call me Arnie,' she said icily, and Dale longed to say she'd do as she pleased, she wasn't Arnie's pupil now.

Trelawney had listened silently to this brief exchange, and now he pushed back his chair and evinced no further interest in Dale's progress in the sewing field.

'I'm going down to the yards,' he said briefly, and went.

A moment passed before Arnoldine said, 'I think you

owe me an apology, Dale.'

Dale looked at her wide-eyed. 'Why? What have I done?'

Arnoldine's attractive face flushed with anger. 'You deliberately tried to make me look small.'

'Oh,' said Dale, her eyes still wide. 'But hadn't you just done the same to me?'

'No, I had not!' Arnie snapped. 'I was taking your part —making excuses for you. I *know* you've been having difficulty with those covers—I've been keeping a check on what you've been doing. And you haven't got very far, have you?'

Dale bit her lip. She couldn't deny that, so perhaps Arnie had been quite sincere, in which case she did owe her an apology.

'I'm sorry then,' she said stiffly. 'All the same, you're quite wrong. I'm not having any difficulties.'

'Then why have you done nothing with the chintz? And why haven't you hung the curtains? Have you made some silly mistake, like cutting them too short or something like that?'

'No, I haven't. I want to make sure Rebie really likes the chintz before I cut into it.'

Arnoldine reached for the coffee jug and poured herself another cup. 'What Rebecca likes or doesn't like is the last thing you need worry about, Dale.'

'I can't think why you should say that,' Dale retorted. 'After all, whether you like it or not, this is going to be her home.'

'I hope not, and I shan't pretend otherwise. You're out of touch, Dale. This world is no longer Rebecca's, and it will be the best thing for everyone concerned if the engagement is broken. If Rebecca can't see it for herself, then I shall do my best to see that Trelawney does.'

'That's—immoral!' exclaimed Dale, shaken. 'You have

no right to interfere when two people love each other.'

Arnoldine laughed shortly.

'Sexual attraction isn't love. Rebecca's thrown herself at his head. And of course he needs a wife—but not one like Rebecca.'

'One like Arnie,' Dale thought. So that *she* would be the person, eventually, whom the furnishings must please.

Well, there was nothing she could do about it all.

CHAPTER EIGHT

REBIE, with Ivor Richards, arrived at Warathar late in the afternoon. Dale hadn't seen a sign of Trelawney since he'd left the breakfast table, and she herself had spent the whole day sewing, working feverishly on the loose covers—not for Arnoldine; for Rebie.

She'd decided to disregard everything Arnoldine had said about the engagement—about Rebie. Obviously her own desires coloured her opinions. She must have been in love with Trelawney years ago and she apparently still was, and Dale had no idea how much encouragement he had given her. It was something she preferred not to think about, but she tried in vain to forget that they had once been lovers. Did he ever—sleepwalk—now? She simply couldn't believe that he did.

She was sickened how, all day, her thoughts circled round and round Trelawney. It was a relief when at last she heard the car and knew that Rebie was there, and she hurried round to the front verandah to greet her.

Arnoldine was there ahead of her, charming in a pale blue V-neck dress, silver ear-rings, silvery sandals. Her dark hair was sheeny and soft, her eyelashes, darkened with mascara, played up the beauty and mystery of her eyes. She was being very hostessy, and Dale heard her asking, 'Did you have much trouble finding your way? Trelawney was quite convinced you'd get lost between one paddock and the next, Rebecca. We didn't know you'd have company, of course ... Oh, here's our other guest. Dale, you've met Ivor Richards, I believe?'

'Hello, Ivor—hello, Rebie.' Dale smiled brightly, but she could see Rebie's blood was boiling at Arnie's mistress-of-the-house act. She was aware that Rebie and Ivor exchanged glances. He looked immaculate in white pants and a red and white striped shirt, while Rebie wore a white skirt, and a white blouse with red coin spots. There was enough similarity between their outfits for Dale to wonder how Arnoldine would interpret it. How was she interpreting it herself, come to that? Almost His and Hers. She felt slightly sick, and any ideas she might have had about carrying Rebie off to inspect the furnishings vanished very rapidly.

'Come along inside and I'll show you your rooms,' Arnoldine said. 'You must be longing to freshen up after that long drive in the hot sun. We'll have cool drinks on the verandah as soon as you like.'

It was too much for Rebie. She snapped out, 'For heaven's sake—I'll have the room I had before. And *I'd* like to decide where Ivor will sleep!'

Arnoldine looked at her with cool amusement. 'Of course you're to have the room you had before, Rebecca,' she soothed. 'But, dear, as the housekeeper, it's my business to get the guest rooms ready.'

Ivor looked slightly uncomfortable, but Rebie glared at Arnoldine ferociously. 'I know you're the *housekeeper*, Arnie. But I'm Trelawney's fiancée, and I'm going to have

things the way *I* want them, not the way you do ... Where's
Trelawney, anyhow?'

'He went out with Murray.' Arnoldine looked so angry
Dale was sure she longed to smack Rebie's face. 'The sale
cattle have to be inoculated before the stock inspector
comes.'

Rebie stared at her. 'Trelawney's down in the yards—
working? I thought he'd broken some ribs. I thought he'd
be lying around somewhere. Resting.'

'Did you? I hardly imagined you knew a thing about
the accident, seeing you stayed away with your friends.'
Arnoldine spoke crisply. 'But don't worry, dear, he's been
well taken care of, and he's promised me he won't over-
exert himself.'

Rebie turned on her heel and went inside, followed by
Ivor, and after a moment Dale went inside too. She didn't
like the situation. Arnoldine, with her more mature years
and experience, had certainly got the better of Rebie. What
on earth did Ivor make of it all? Dale wondered unhappily.
And what kind of game was Rebie playing?

Inside, she could hear Rebie and Ivor conversing in low
tones, and she didn't have the nerve to join them. Instead
she went right through the house and stood on the back
verandah, staring into the garden through the peperina
trees with their feathery green leaves. Clouds were piling
up in the sky as they did every evening, and the air was
oppressively hot and seemed charged with electricity—in
more ways than one. Dale leaned against the verandah
post, feeling exhausted and rather depressed. She had
waited and waited for Rebie, and now Rebie didn't seem
particularly interested in her. As well, she had the feeling
there was trouble ahead.

A few minutes later, as she stood there, her eye was
caught by a movement among the trees, and she saw Ivor

and Rebie moving among the shadows. Rebie had changed into a long loose cotton dress, and as Dale watched, she raised her face to Ivor and he drew her against him and kissed her lingeringly.

Dale wasn't sure what she felt. She turned away quickly, wishing she hadn't seen that embrace. How could Rebie be so blatantly disloyal? Or didn't engagements matter all that much any more? Yet to kiss someone else was not, after all, being unfaithful. The trouble was that she was too much of an idealist—a purist—when it came to love. Though that might be hard to guess from some of her behaviour lately!

When she turned again, Trelawney had appeared at the other end of the garden, Rebie and Ivor had emerged from the trees, and were walking towards him as if nothing at all had happened. If Trelawney had seen what she had seen, Dale thought, then it didn't show. They all greeted each other, Trelawney kissed Rebie, shook Ivor by the hand, and then they all came back towards the house.

Dale slipped silently into the sewing room and closed the door softly behind her. She heard the others come on to the verandah, heard Rebie say something about drinks. 'I'll be fifteen minutes,' said Trelawney. 'I need a shower.'

When the voices had faded away, Dale emerged and went into the garden. She had begun to think that there were two men in love with Rebie—and to wonder which of them Rebie loved the most. Was she opting for Trelawney simply to prevent Arnie from having him? Or was she merely enjoying a little flirtation with Ivor before she was married and tied up forever?

Well, there was no point in trying to work it all out.

Dale walked down to the waterhole, and there she paused in the shade of the big white gums and leaned back against a smooth tree trunk. She watched some white cockatoos

flying about in the branches above, but no matter how she
tried she couldn't get her mind off the tangled relation-
ships that were being worked out at Warathar. She fitted
nowhere into the picture. She was no more than a passer-by
who had strolled on to the stage in the middle of a play.
And fallen in love with the leading man, she confessed
wryly to herself.

She'd have to go away, of course—start her own life
again.

She didn't know how long she'd been standing among
the trees when she saw Trelawney coming down to the
water. She straightened guiltily. They must be having their
drinks on the verandah and wondering where she was——

'I'm here, Trelawney,' she called, certain he hadn't seen
her yet. 'Are you looking for me?'

She watched him as he came towards her, conscious of
the gleam on his tawny hair, the breadth of his shoulders,
the narrowness of his hips in the dark pants he wore. She
had become achingly familiar with the sight of him, though
she hadn't been alone with him since that evening by the
homestead swimming pool. And now her heart had begun
to pound, and she felt desire rise in her wildly and unexpectedly, like a gush of water from an underground
spring. She burned to feel his mouth against hers, to have
his body hard against her own, and it was utterly shaming.
Turning away from the sight of him, she leaned trem-
blingly against the tree trunk once more.

'So this is where you're hiding,' he said, halting near her
and looking at her half mockingly through lashes that had
the same bright sheen as his hair. 'I wasn't looking for you,
as a matter of fact—I just came down here to enjoy the
peace of my kingdom.' He rested one hand on the tree
trunk near her shoulder, and he looked not at her, now,
but at the waters of the lagoon.

Dale felt rather foolish—abashed that she'd imagined he'd come to look for her. She said jerkily, 'I thought you'd come to tell me it was time to join the others. I—I apologise for being here and disturbing your peace,' she added.

'You're not disturbing my peace—at least not the way you mean, Daisy,' he said enigmatically. 'It would take more than an innocent girl to do that. Since the old man died, I've been able to drink my fill of this land—this land that I love more than life. It's been a long exile, but it's over now, thank God.' He spoke broodingly, almost as if he were talking to himself, and though he had once before told her that his affinity was here, she hadn't realised that he meant it so deeply until just now, when she could hear it in his voice, see it in the darkening of his eyes that were usually so hard. But as for his exile, even though he had left Jackalass so that Arnoldine might stay, he'd been in trouble even before that, with Stephanie, Ray's wife-to-be. 'Kissing' her was how Rebie had put it, and even if there had been nothing else, Dale knew from personal experience how dangerous his kisses could be.

Now she couldn't resist saying a little cynically, 'It was your own fault you were exiled, though, wasn't it?'

He looked at her questioningly along his shoulder.

'Exactly what do you mean by that disapproving remark? Are you pointing a moral and suggesting I deserved exile as a punishment for my wicked indulgence? I was not much older than you are now, you know. You might give me credit for having been at least a little in love,' he finished with a crooked smile.

Dale bit her lip. It was true she didn't ever really think of him as having been in love with Arnoldine. That old image she had of him as a wild young man kept getting in the way, and now she just didn't know what he felt. But the affair with Stephanie was rather different, and she told him with a cool little smile, 'I wasn't thinking so much of Arnie. I was thinking of what happened *here*—of why you had to leave Warathar and go to Jackalass.'

'And what the hell would you know about that?' He was obviously taken aback.

'Oh, we all knew about you and Stephanie,' she said carelessly and inaccurately, because she wasn't going to admit the story had been whispered to her by Rebie. 'It was no wonder your uncle didn't want you on the place.'

'Well, that's one way of looking at it,' he said dryly. 'But my own desires and decisions came into it too. Even at twenty-two I wasn't unrealistic enough to imagine I had much chance of winning Stephanie back. Come to that, I didn't really want to. I was in a position rather similar to yours, but I reacted to it differently. She dropped me when she met Ray. He was the better proposition—older, established, more sophisticated—and she decided to do something about it and succeeded. It was all very practical, very cerebral, but it came off and she's stuck to him, and as far as I know they're quite happy together, and I bear her no ill-will. At the time, however, I was in love with her. That was why I left Warathar and set about getting her out of my system as fast as I could.'

Dale listened with bewilderment. It appeared that Stephanie had been his girl-friend in the first place. And was he implying that his affair with Arnoldine had been undertaken to help him forget the other girl? She said slowly, 'I always thought that Stephanie was engaged to Ray and that you—you——'

He sent her a smile that was not very pleasant. 'You thought I set out to have an affair with her? You certainly must have had some unflattering ideas about me in those days, young Daisy! The simple truth of the matter is that I invited Stephanie here and when she met Ray she changed her mind about me. There's nothing so wrong about that in actual fact. She was free and so was he, and lots of girls have an eye to the main chance. Heart doesn't always rule the head by any means. And as you know from your own experience, it's not only girls who can change their minds. For one reason or another most human beings switch from one love to another before they even attempt to settle down ... Not a very profound statement, and I hope you'll excuse me if we leave it there. I didn't come down to the waterhole to indulge in argument or discussion.'

Dale moved uneasily. His talk of changing one's mind, of switching from one love to another had just too many relevancies at this moment in time, and she had no wish to extend it any further. She said with a wry smile, 'I'm sorry I started it. I've disturbed your peace after all, haven't I?'

He gave her a long smouldering look that disturbed her deeply. 'Darling, don't you know yet that you always do that?' His glance moved over her slowly, down the length of her figure, and then returned to her face and the clarity of her amber-hazel eyes. 'Every time I set eyes on you, Daisy, I think to myself, Good Good, does that girl still think she's in a state of mourning? How *is* your broken heart, anyway? We haven't discussed it lately—and aren't going to now, I have no doubt you're all ready to tell me.'

As he spoke he took his hand from the tree trunk and idly lifted a strand of her hair from her temple. At his touch, she felt her pulses quicken and she answered him nervously.

'You—you should know one doesn't get over a love affair in a few weeks. Not when it's been so——' She hesitated. She'd been going to insist that her love affair had been real, intense. And she had believed that, yet now the fact was she'd scarcely spared a thought for Andrew in what seemed like ages. But that might be too revealing a fact to admit to Trelawney Saber and she stumbled on incoherently, 'It—it takes a long time to forget——'

'That's negative thinking,' he said mockingly. 'There are ways of speeding up the process, and one is to fall in love again—which is what we've been talking about, to some extent.'

His hand had slid down to her shoulder, and Dale stared down at the lagoon where the dragonflies were skimming along with their watery reflections. If Trelawney only knew, she'd done exactly as he recommended, though it certainly hadn't done her much good. She'd emerged from a girlish infatuation to fall into the midst of a futile passion for a man who had no tender feelings for her whatsoever. Even now, she was so acutely aware of the weight of his hand on her shoulder that it was making her breath quicken.

Scarcely knowing what she was saying, she told him, 'I don't want to—to fall in love with anyone else, thank you. I——'

'You prefer to dramatise yourself, do you? To wallow in the memory of a romance that as far as I can gather never even grew wings. And now, like some exhibitionist, you're busy protecting yourself from male attentions by wearing those unlovely clothes ... Tell me, Daisy, do you wear black bra and knickers too?'

Her eyelids flickered up with shock—and of course he'd meant to shock her. His face was only inches away and his hand moved on her shoulder till his fingers were under the shoulderstrap of her black vest. Her heart had begun to bang with fright, and with a mad and shameful excitement as well. She could feel his fingers burningly on her bare skin. 'Touch me—kiss me—love me,' a voice inside her cried urgently, and her whole body seemed to throb with desire for him. She felt quite incapable of rational thought, and it was only with an immense effort of will that she managed to stay where she was, leaning passively against the tree trunk as if nothing he did or said mattered to her. Yet she couldn't make herself look away from him. Her gaze remained locked with his, and in his eyes she saw a dark savagery, as if he wanted to hurt her.

'If you belonged to me,' he said after a moment, and his teeth showed white against the deep tan of his skin, 'I'd soon teach you not to go around looking like that.'

'If I belonged to you?' she exclaimed, paling. 'What an incredible thing to say! Girls don't—don't think like that in these days of—of liberation.'

'Maybe some girls don't. But you're hardly the epitome of the liberated female, are you, Daisy?' He raised one eyebrow quizzically and her glance moved momentarily to the scar on his cheek. 'Anyhow, you could do with a little instruction, darling.'

'From you, I suppose,' she said huskily. She wished he'd take his hand from her shoulder, but she wasn't going to ask him to. Even though his fingers were still, she was disturbingly aware of their warmth, their male texture. 'Well, I don't want you to teach me a thing——'

'What on earth do you think we're talking about?' he asked his eyes mocking. 'Sex?'

Dale stared at him speechlessly. Of course that was what they were talking about, but apparently not, for he continued flatly, 'We're talking about clothes—about dressing, don't you remember? This sort of thing——' With a rough unexpected movement, he pushed the sleeve of her vest down from her shoulder. Then she heard his sharply indrawn breath and his hand slid to her breast.

'Daisy——' His eyes sought and found hers, and her

heart beat against his hand. His lips parted softly, she closed her eyes then opened them to look back into his, and she felt the movement of his body towards hers.

'Oh God,' he muttered on a groan. The male roughness of his skin came against her forehead, she smelt the tingling scent of the after-shave lotion he used—at odds with and yet so much a part of his masculinity. Passion rocked along her nerves as he lowered his head and put his mouth against the softness of her throat. The touch of his lips, intimate, caressing, roused her to an expectancy that was sheer madness. She was sick with desire by the time he left her throat alone and sought her mouth, one hand coming to the small of her back so she was drawn close against his body. She heard the hum of insects, the sound of wings as birds began to come down to the lagoon, and all the restless brooding heat, the aching bigness of summer seemed to invade her body. Something within her was waiting to burst into flame, into flower, into life, as she stood there locked in his arms.

'Your—chest,' she heard herself whisper faintly against the mouth that moved so caressingly, so sensuously against her own. But if Trelawney felt any discomfort, he seemed completely unaware of it as his passion rose and his hand slid inside the waistband of her jeans to lie against the smoothness of her belly.

'Oh God, Daisy, I want you so much,' he muttered.

He withdrew from her abruptly and thrusting his hands in his pockets strode across the red earth to stand by the waters of the lagoon, now turning a metallic red as the slanting rays of the setting sun forced their way through the piled up clouds.

For minutes, Dale was in too much of a turmoil to think at all. She leaned limply back against the tree, her eyes on the back of the man who was causing so much havoc in her life. Why did this sort of thing have to happen between them? It was his fault—it wasn't hers, she told herself feverishly. Oh, she wanted it—she wanted more than he ever gave her. But she wouldn't invite it, she couldn't. Sharply the memory of Rebie came back. His fiancée— who had been in Ivor Richards' arms. But that was no excuse for anything. It might perhaps explain Trelawney's behaviour to some extent. If he had seen those two kissing, he could be feeling sore and savage enough to retaliate. Yet it wasn't an explanation that satisfied her.

Feeling restless, frustrated, guilty, she watched a pelican sail tranquilly across the water, disturbing the green tree shadows. She watched motionless, sure that *he* was watching it too, wondering what he was feeling, wondering who he was thinking about—her or Rebie. Then quietly she began to walk back to the homestead.

She didn't look back to see if he were following her, but she walked fast as if to escape from him. What they had done was wrong and it was dangerous. She couldn't see it any other way—and that was because she was—hardly the epitome of the liberated female ...

At the homestead she went straight to her room, thankful that she met no one on the way. There, she looked at herself in the mirror and discovered that she was crying and that she looked white and sick and scared—also desperately unattractive. So why had Trelawney bothered with her? It was pathetic, she thought bitterly, wiping her tears away. Pathetic and *funny*. That Trelawney Saber, with his maturity, his sophistication, should take time off to get worked up over her, Daisy Driscoll. Over her unappealing, but nevertheless feminine, physical being. It must have something to do with Rebie's behaviour, that was all, though she didn't understand now and she didn't suppose she ever would. She just knew it mustn't happen again, that she mustn't let it. She was well aware that Trelawney was a passionate man, and the one absolutely infallible method of not getting mixed up with him was to keep away from him. This evening, she should have had more sense than to stay and talk to him. She should have left him to his peace, his contemplation or whatever, and come straight up to the house. Then nothing would have happened.

Nothing. The word echoed painfully in her heart.

Swallowing a sob, she snatched up her toilet things and went to the bathroom. Under the shower, she let the luke-warm water run soothingly over her burning body—washing away her tears, washing away the touch of his hands. She wasn't really in love with him, she told herself determinedly. It was just a physical attraction of some kind and he was unscrupulous enough to cash in on it. Or perhaps he imagined he was helping her to get over Andrew—which he was, with a vengeance! It was probably a game he knew backwards, though she suspected he didn't altogether know how successfully he was playing it in this case.

Oh God, how was she going to get through the rest of the evening?

In her room she got into the beige pants and a checked shirt, and persuaded her hair to curl a little. Her tears didn't show unless you looked very hard, and she hoped no one would be interested enough to do that.

They weren't. Not even Arnie. And Dale discovered it was not so hard after all to sit through dinner. Looking normal, at least as far as dress was concerned, helped quite a lot, and it helped still more—though it hurt quite damnably—that Trelawney practically ignored her. Over dinner, in fact, he and Rebie were very much the engaged couple, and later they went to walk in the garden together.

Dale excused herself and went to bed leaving Arnie with

Ivor and the jackaroo and not caring much what any of them thought about her.

The three men went out early the next morning. The stock inspector was expected, and arrangements had been made for the sale cattle to be taken to the railhead at Julia Creek. As well, according to Arnoldine who knew everything, the two big trucks were expected back from their first trip, with supplies they'd been picking up before the Wet began. Dale at last brought up the subject of the furnishings with Rebie.

'I've been making some curtains, Rebie. You did get my note, didn't you?'

'Yes, but honestly, Daisy, you don't have to kill yourself over that business.'

Dale frowned. 'I'm not killing myself, but I've made a start. As a matter of fact, I thought you'd picked out the fabrics and decided on colour schemes and all that kind of thing. I hope you'll be pleased with what I've done so far —just some curtains for the sitting room, and I've started on the chairs. Trelawney more or less told me what he— er—thought you'd want.'

'Well, let's see them,' said Rebie without a great deal of enthusiasm, and they both made their way to the sewing room.

'Fine—the curtains look fine,' she told Dale after a brief inspection. 'As for the chair covers, you're a marvel! I couldn't do that kind of thing in a million years.'

'Oh, you could if you really tried. Arnie would help you——'

'I don't want Arnie's help,' Rebie said shortly. 'In fact, what I'd like most would be for her to buzz off somewhere else and stop trying to make herself a fixture at Warathar. She hangs on and on, just like a leech.'

Dale looked at her worriedly. 'What will you do about her after you're married?'

Rebie walked restlessly across the room and back again without answering. 'How has she been behaving since you've been here?' she asked abruptly.

Dale felt uncomfortable. She didn't know what to say, but she certainly wasn't going to pass on the remarks Arnie had made about Rebie. She said at last, 'She's managed everything very well. She's a good housekeeper, you know—everything's been running very smoothly. And she's—she'd more or less kept an eye on Trelawney's fracture.'

Rebie snorted. 'I'll bet she's done that! But I don't give a hang if she's the world's best housekeeper. What I mean is, has she been gunning for Trelawney?'

'I don't think so,' said Dale, not wanting to make trouble. 'She drove him out to the camp—and for the mail—but someone had to do that, he can't really drive with any degree of comfort yet, and he doesn't like *my* driving much. Anyhow, he's asked you to marry him, so there'd hardly be any point in her—hoping for anything, would there?' she finished brightly.

'Oh, she'll never give up hoping,' Rebie said cynically. 'She would just love to reign supreme over this cattle station. Thank goodness you've been here—that must have put a brake on her activities.'

Dale turned away, her cheeks scarlet. She'd hate Rebie to know some of the things that had been happening between herself and Trelawney.

'Shall we get on with the sewing now you're here?' she asked, changing the subject. 'And we really must hang those curtains—they oughtn't to be hemmed till they've been up for a few days and allowed to drop.'

'Okay, let's hang the curtains,' Rebie agreed with a

grimace. 'But I'm not going to mess about with anything else. After all, the Richards have only a few more days of their holiday left. They'll be going back to Brisbane soon, and I can hardly be stitching away when they're expecting tennis or swimming. Ivor's coming back to the house for lunch, and this afternoon we'll go out to the pool and maybe have some tennis later on if it cools off a bit. Trelawney can't play, I suppose, but you will, won't you? If Murray knocks off early enough he might join us too, otherwise I suppose we'll have to ask Arnie. Cut-throat's a bit too strenuous for me.'

'Yes, I'll play,' Dale agreed, gathering up the curtains and preparing to lead the way to the sitting room. 'By the way, is there something going on between Murray and Buff? He seems very nice—and he had a letter from her.'

'Oh, Buff will write to anyone,' Rebie said dismissively. 'She thinks he's a nice guy too, and that's all.'

'Is it? I rather got the feeling there was more to it than that—and I suspect Trelawney thinks so too.'

'Well, perhaps he's in love with her,' Rebie agreed crossly, 'but she's not in love with him. She's always been——' She stopped, obviously changing her mind about what she'd been going to say. 'I know Buff better than you do, Daisy, and she'll never marry Murray Hewson, that's all. Now come on and let's get rid of these damned curtains.'

Dale complied, but she felt puzzled and disturbed, as well as being just a little hurt at Rebie's lack of gratitude. She didn't seem at all interested in the redecorating of the home that would be hers. In fact, she seemed more interested in enjoying herself. With Ivor Richards...

The rest of the day proceeded as Rebie had planned, and Dale joined in, abandoning the sewing, and wondering if Rebie really wanted her around. In a day or two, she thought, Kevin and Philippa would swell the party and it would all be a lot less awkward. But Rebie, after her initial lapse, showed no signs of being more than good friends with Ivor, so it was a case of the good old platonic friendship after all, Dale reassured herself, though not very convincingly. She made up her mind that when the others re-returned to Jackalass, she'd go with them, with or without Rebie. She wasn't going to stay on here for any reason at all, especially as Rebie didn't seem interested in the sewing.

Beyond her return to Jackalass she didn't look. Not yet. Not till she had to.

CHAPTER NINE

THREE uneventful days went by, and Dale wondered why she'd ever thought Rebie might be having an affair with Ivor. Quite positively she wasn't. She devoted herself to Trelawney—when he was there. Which was mainly in the evenings. He was apparently feeling much better, since he spent most of the day with the cattle.

Ivor went out with the men in the mornings, but he came home at lunch time and spent the afternoon with the girls. Dale found him pleasant, and though she suspected he might be at least a little in love with Rebie, he never made the least attempt to get her to himself. Whatever Arnie said, Dale began to feel the marriage was going to happen and it was going to work.

It was a Saturday when Kevin and Philippa turned up, and everyone congregated on the verandah for drinks before dinner. Dale, having discovered the other girls were dressing up, rather nervously put on the green brocade. It was surprising how different she looked—very slender, older, the colour of her eyes picking up the green of the dress. The weather had become almost unbearably humid and she'd have been more comfortable in cotton, but that couldn't be helped. At least she looked good, she thought, as she went on to the verandah to join the group there.

The men were already drinking glasses of ice-cold beer, and the light that flooded the verandah from beneath the awnings gilded everything it struck with vibrant colour.

'Wet'll come early this year,' Kevin remarked in his pleasant drawl as Dale dropped down in a chair near Rebie. Murray, who already knew her tastes, handed her a glass of home-made lemonade garnished with a sprig of mint. 'I reckon we'd better scoot back to Jackalass tomorrow evening,' Kevin continued. 'Still a lot to be done if we want to beat the rain. Sorry about that, folks. I know you'd enjoy the swimming here, Pip, but there it is—and I want to see all of you I can before you go back to Brissie. I guess you'll stay here, Rebie. And what about you, Daisy?' he added, smiling across at her. 'What are your plans?'

'I'll have to be going too,' she said. She set down her glass and twisted her fingers together nervously, and didn't look in Trelawney's direction.

'Oh, you can't go yet, Daisy,' Rebie exclaimed. 'We've seen practically nothing of each other. I don't see why you —and Ivor—and I shouldn't stay a few more days. You don't want me to come back and do your housekeeping, do you, Kev?'

'Can't say I do,' Kevin said with a grin. 'Pip's been managing beautifully, besides which I have a surprise for everyone. Buff rang through from Charters Towers last night. She'll be back home at Jackalass in a week or so. Asked me to let you know, Murray,' he finished, giving the jackaroo a friendly smile.

'Do you mean she's leaving poor David on his own?' Arnoldine said accusingly as she refilled Trelawney's glass.

'No, she's found someone to come in and housekeep for Dad,' Kevin explained. 'He'll be well looked after.'

Dale saw Ivor give Rebie a rather odd glance before Arnoldine said scornfully, 'For how long, I wonder? It's not as easy as all that to get hold of a good housekeeper who can be depended on to stay.'

'Oh, for goodness' sake, Arnie!' Rebie exclaimed rudely. 'You're not the only good housekeeper in Queensland. Buff will have made sure Daddy's going to be in good hands, don't you worry.' She turned back to her brother. 'Did you say anything to Buff about Trelawney and me?'

'As a matter of fact, no, I didn't. I wasn't sure if you'd told them or not, and as that's your particular privilege, I shut up. Have you told Dad, by the way?' He looked from Rebie to Trelawney, who leaned back in his chair and said indolently, 'Have you told your father, Rebie?'

'Well—no,' she admitted. 'I haven't got around to it yet, what with this and that.' She left her chair and went to stand against the verandah rails, her back to the light. 'It can wait till Buff's here, anyhow.'

'We'll make a joint announcement,' said Kevin after a moment. 'Pip and I have decided we'll get married after Christmas.' He reached out and took the hand of the pretty girl who sat beside him, and they looked at each other and smiled, and Dale envied them.

'That calls for congratulations and a celebration,' Trelawney remarked. 'You think you'll be happy out here in our wilderness?' he asked Philippa.

'I'm sure of it,' she said with quiet confidence. 'And it's not a wilderness. I love it. We only decided this morning, so I haven't told my parents yet either.' She looked at her brother, her eyes sparkling. 'D'you think I'll have their blessing, Ivor? If Mother looks like having the vapours, will you assure her it's all very civilised?'

'Certainly—if that'll make you happy,' he agreed, and Dale thought, '*He* doesn't like it here. *He* thinks it's a wilderness.' All these love matches, she was thinking. She hadn't missed the implication of Buff's special message for Murray. Rebie was wrong—the love wasn't only on his side ...

Dinner that night became a celebration. Champagne was produced and toasts were drunk, not only to Pip and Kevin, but to Rebie and Trelawney too, on Kevin's suggestion. Dale, glancing covertly at Ivor, was aware he wasn't delighted. All the same, it seemed that Arnie was way off beam, and Dale smiled brightly and lifted her glass. Inside, she was slowly but surely going to pieces and she hoped the champagne would hold her together. Nothing had finally been decided as to who was leaving for Jackalass tomorrow and who was staying, and after dinner Dale made an opportunity to ask Rebie, as they moved on to the comparative coolness of the verandah, 'What about tomorrow, Rebie? I really think I should go.'

'Oh, nonsense,' Rebie said quickly. 'Tree's quite happy to have any number of people staying here. And if Ivor's to stay, then you must stay too. You'd both be mad to go to Jackalass when the pool here's such a life-saver. That's one thing I will say about Warathar ... What's your hurry, anyhow? You don't have a job to go back to. Is it a man?'

'Yes,' said Dale after a moment. It was a man—but a man she had to get away from.

'Oh.' Rebie was disconcerted. 'Oh well, a few more days aren't going to hurt, are they? Ivor wants to stay here, and besides, it will give Kev and Pip a few more days on their own.'

'Well—all right,' Dale said reluctantly. She glanced along the verandah to where Trelawney was standing, talking to Ivor, and he raised his eyes and looked back at her exactly as if she'd called his name. It was enough to send her senses spinning, and she despaired of herself.

Later that night as she was coming from the bathroom on her way to bed, she encountered Trelawney in the hallway. He stood blocking her way quite deliberately, and she stopped and looked at him, her heart beating fast, her face losing its colour.

'You've snapped out of it lately with your new image, Daisy,' he remarked. 'You're making quite an impression on the males in the household.'

'Thank you. But I don't believe you,' she said dryly. 'I suppose you think it will do my ego good to be complimented.'

'Maybe. How is your ego, anyhow? Does it match up to your new appearance?'

'What do you mean?'

'Have you decided to take my advice and come to terms with your broken heart? Is it, in fact, on the mend? You've been talking about leaving—I'd be interested to hear what you plan to do.'

'I'll go back to Rockhampton,' she said briefly. She would have to go there to collect her things from Sally's flat, so that was true enough. As to whether she would stay there, look for work, she didn't know. The idea of running into Andrew didn't disturb her badly any more, but she had the idea she was going to need new surroundings, new interests—to help get her over another love affair; and this time, she thought glumly, it was going to take a lot longer.

'And when do you plan to go?' One hand resting on his hip, Trelawney was studying her intently.

'Rebie wants me to stay a few more days—till Ivor has to go. Will that be all right?'

'Sure. I'm not trying to push you out. Do you intend to look up your boy-friend again? Or is that all over?'

Her eyes fell before his. 'I don't know,' she said indistinctly, and when she looked up again his lips were compressed and he was frowning.

'Listen, Daisy,' he said after a moment. 'I'm going to suggest you do look him up. You might find you've changed. I hope you do, but you certainly ought to find out. I'll be coming over to the coast in January. I'll see you then, and you can tell me how it's worked out. Have you got that? I'll want your address, of course.'

Dale listened tensely. She didn't need to see Andrew again to discover she'd changed. And if Trelawney would be on the coast in January, did that mean he and Rebie had fixed their wedding date for some time then?

She forced herself to say brightly, 'Oh, I'll be giving my address to Rebie, naturally. I don't want to miss out on an invitation to the wedding!' What a lie! She knew it would be like death to go to the wedding.

His eyes narrowed slightly and their glances locked. Dale found it hard to look away. That tawny hair, those greenish eyes, the shadow on his cheek that was a scar—the indentations at the corners of his mouth. She knew them all by heart, yet not sufficiently so. She wanted to look at him for hours so that she would be able to visualise him in detail for ever.

Trelawney's glance shifted first, and he said, 'I like your dress. It's not Arnoldine's, but the stuff looks vaguely familiar. Where did you get it?' For a second she thought he was going to reach out and touch the silky material, but instead he put his hands in the pockets of his dark pants and looked at her enigmatically.

'I made it,' she said. 'I'm afraid I took the stuff from the store—and some shirts and a pair of jeans too. I'll pay for them all, of course.'

'Forget it,' he said shortly.

They were both silent. The house was quiet, the only sound faint music from Rebie's room, where she was playing her transistor radio as she did every night.

Dale moved. 'Well—goodnight.'

'Goodnight, Daisy.'

She stepped past him quickly, her arm brushing against the material of his cream shirt. A minute electric shock seemed to go through her, her step faltered for an instant, then she continued on her way. Shamingly, she knew she wanted Trelawney to reach out for her, and she felt sick with disappointment that he didn't. She hungered for his touch, yet she was going to have to do without it for ever.

In her room she shut the door and stood in the hot darkness, her heart beating suffocatingly fast. Under the brocade dress she wore only panties and bra, and she felt so aware of her body and its desires it was frightening. Undoing her dress, she stepped out of it and felt the warm air flow over her body. The crazy thought went through her head that on her wedding night, Rebie would be undressing like this for Trelawney. In January. So soon! Would she torture herself by going to the wedding? Or would she torture herself by staying away? She had no idea. Her fingers trembled as she unfastened her bra, and she was no longer thinking of Rebie. She was imagining herself as Trelawney's bride—feeling his arms around her as he lifted her and carried her to the bed, whispering words of love in her ear——

'Daisy Driscoll, you are off your head!' she told herself,

as with a determined movement she crossed the room and groped under the pillow for her pyjamas. She wasn't going to fantasise, it was weak, it was morally bad, and seconds later she lay under the sheet, her eyes closed, her limbs straight, concentrating on relaxing, and wishing she were leaving tomorrow evening with Kevin and Pip.

After Kevin and Philippa had gone, life at Warathar returned to the familiar routine of the week before—the swimming, the tennis, the electric storms at night. The nights grew hotter and more humid, and though Dale blamed her sleeplessness on that, she knew it had other, deeper causes. Everyone seemed a little moody, a little touchy, even Ivor, who finally gave up spending his mornings on the run with the other men.

Dale was treated to a lecture from Arnoldine on Buff's lack of consideration for her father, to which she replied that she supposed Buff had her own reasons for wanting to come back to Jackalass.

'I'm sure she'll have found someone suitable to look after Uncle David, anyhow,' she said, and as she spoke it occurred to her that *she* could go and look after him if necessary. But no—it would be madness. It would keep her in too close touch with the rest of the family—with Rebie and Trelawney and the pain in her heart.

With stunning suddenness, the day for herself and Ivor to leave arrived. They were to drive to Jackalass in Dale's car, and Rebie was to stay at Warathar. That was taken for granted. Murray as usual had left the homestead soon after sun-up, but Trelawney had stayed to see his guests and say farewell to them before he too joined the stockmen in the paddocks.

He shook hands with Dale in the dining room when

breakfast was over, then leaned down and brushed his lips against her cheek.

'Don't forget to leave your Rockhampton address with us,' he reminded her, and she nodded.

'Oh yes—for the wedding invitation,' she heard herself say, her head swimming with sleeplessness and the emotional strain of the moment. Then to her relief he turned to Ivor to say goodbye to him.

Later, from her bedroom, she saw him cross the garden on his way to the horse paddock. He had been taking quite an active part on the station for some days now, and she concluded his ribs must be well on the mend, though he still kept them strapped up. When he had disappeared, she began listlessly to pack her belongings. They were to leave straight after lunch, spend the night at Jackalass, and then make an early start for the coast—she in her own car, the Richards in theirs. Rebie had suggested a morning at the pool, but evidently Arnoldine was not joining them, for Dale had seen her lying in the shade on the verandah, reading, her feet up on the cane lounger. The humid weather was evidently bothering her, for she hadn't been in the best of humours lately. Of course it must be plain to her now that there was nothing she could do to come between Trelawney and Rebie. Ivor had behaved in an exemplary manner apart from that initial lapse. He too must see that Rebie had set her heart on marrying Trelawney, Dale reflected, getting into her bikini. She wondered again what Arnoldine would do and where she'd go once the marriage was an accomplished fact. Probaly Arnoldine was wondering the same thing herself...

Ivor was already in the water when Dale and Rebie walked round to the pool. Dale dived in as soon as she'd shed her sandals, and when she surfaced Ivor was pulling himself out on to the tiles near where Rebie stood, her blue maillot emphasising her curves, and showing up her lovely long legs. Ivor spoke to her, and after a slight hesitation, instead of joining Dale in the water, she went with him towards the palms. There, both of them stretched out on the grass, Rebie on her side, Ivor on his stomach, his head turned towards the girl.

They were talking, Dale noticed, as she swam and floated and tried not to think that, unless she went to his wedding, she would never see Trelawney Saber again. She didn't know how long she'd been in the water when, as she swam slowly the length of the pool, she saw Ivor get to his feet and with an angry-looking gesture sling his towel over his shoulder. Rebie sat up and stared at him, her cheeks flushed. Dale had the feeling they'd been quarrelling, but it was nothing to do with her if they had. At all events, she was going to keep out of the way. She reached the end of the pool, turned, and swam back again.

When finally she saw him striding off towards the house, she left the water. Rebie, leaning back on her hands, watched her moodily as she stooped for her towel.

'I'd better go inside and dress,' said Dale, beginning to rub her hair dry.

'No—wait. Come over here, I want to talk to you.'

Rebie spoke so abruptly and so strangely that Dale stared at her in surprise, and discovered her moody look had turned to one that bordered on tears.

'What's the matter, Rebie?' Concerned, Dale dropped down on the grass beside her, and Rebie turned her face aside and hugged her knees.

'Listen, Daisy—everything's changed. You—you're not going with Ivor today.'

'But I must!' Dale exclaimed, taken aback. 'It's all been arranged. I've—I've said goodbye to Trelawney—— What on earth are you talking about?'

'I've told you, it's all been changed. *I'm* going with Ivor —in my car.'

Dale couldn't make sense of it. 'Does Trelawney know?' she asked bewilderedly.

'No, of course not. I just decided now. It's this heat— the humidity,' she hurried on. 'I just can't take any more of it. I've got the hell of a headache.'

'I'm sorry,' said Dale with a frown. 'It's up to you if you go, of course, but I'm leaving too. I can't stay—particularly not if you're leaving. I mean, after all——' Her voice trailed off.

Rebie turned her head and looked at her exasperatedly. She hadn't shed any tears, and no longer looked like doing so. 'Why can't you stay? And why shouldn't you? You were here with just Arnie and Tree before Ivor and I arrived.'

'Yes, but that was because I was waiting for you. And it was better to be here than at Jackalass. But if you're going to Jackalass, then of course I'm coming too.'

'Oh, talk sense, Daisy,' Rebie said tiredly. 'Why would I stay at Jackalass? I'm going over to the coast to get away from this stinking climate. It doesn't bother you all that much by the look of you, but I'm wrung out ... Daisy, you've just *got* to stay! You don't think I'm going to leave Trelawney completely at Arnie's mercy—*now*?'

'But why should you worry about Arnie now?' Dale asked, confusedly. 'After all, you're being married in January.'

Rebie stared. 'Where did you get hold of that idea? We haven't set a date—not even a time of year—and that's the trouble. If Arnie so much as suspects that anything's wrong, she'll be after Tree like a pack of hounds. You *must* stay, Daisy—to hold the fort.'

'But how on earth can I do that?' Dale protested, any

calm she had attained in the pool completely shattered by now. 'And—and for how long?'

'Oh you can keep up appearances,' Rebie said vaguely. 'Carry on with the damned furnishings,' she added with sudden inspiration. 'Just as if—just till Buff comes,' she concluded, her blue eyes suddenly veiled.

'Now you're not making sense,' Dale said crossly. She'd made up her mind she was leaving and she wasn't altering her plans because of some hare-brained scheme of Rebie's. 'Buff won't be coming here—except to see Murray, I suppose.'

'Oh Murray,' Rebie said dismissively, and added illogically, 'There you are then—she will be coming here. We'll call in at Charters Towers, anyhow, and I'll explain to her.'

'Explain what? Oh—about your engagement, you mean. She doesn't know yet, does she? But honestly, Rebie, I can't see any point in all this, and—and I just don't *want* to stay here any longer.'

'Oh God!' Rebie exclaimed. She pushed her light brown hair back from her face with a nervous hand, then said tensely, 'If you really must know it all, Daisy, the engagement's off. It's finished. I didn't want to tell you, but if you're going to make difficulties——'

Dale had gone pale and she felt as if she were about to faint. She couldn't have heard correctly—she couldn't! The engagement was off. When had it happened—and why didn't anyone know? And why should *she* stay here? She said dazedly, 'I don't understand, Rebie. You—did *you* break off the engagement?'

Rebie sighed. 'Actually, no. In fact, as far as everyone else is concerned—except you and me—and Ivor,' she added after a fractional pause, 'it's still on.'

'But—Trelawney—you haven't told *Trelawney*?' Dale's eyes widened in disbelief.

'No, I haven't, and I'm not going to. It's best he shouldn't know till Buff comes. *She* can tell him. That's what I'm going to explain to her—or part of it, anyhow. And for heaven's sake, Daisy, stop looking like a half-stunned duck. Look, if I tell you, I can trust you, can't I? You won't breathe a word to anyone?'

Dale shook her head. 'Of course I won't, not if you don't want me to. But if you go, how on earth are you going to explain it to Trelawney or to—to anyone?'

'I've thought of that,' said Rebie. 'You can tell him I've lost my contact lenses. We'll tell Arnie that too. God knows I'm helpless without them, and I didn't bring my glasses with me, I just never wear them now. I've got these new things. I'll leave a note for Tree—I can make my handwriting cock-eyed enough to be convincing. I'll say I'll be back as soon as possible.'

'But you won't be back?'

'No, of course not. I've told you that, haven't I?'

Dale looked at her sombrely. 'Why are you breaking it off, Rebie? Don't you want to marry him? Don't you—don't you love him?'

'No,' Rebie said flatly. 'I never even meant to get engaged to him. It just—happened. There seemed nothing else to do. Oh, he's quite a masterpiece,' she conceded wryly, 'but he's far too uncompromisingly masculine for my tastes—he and his damned Gulf country. I never even have a clue what he's thinking about. You know what I mean? In Brissie, men are just other human beings—the men I mix with, that is. You can communicate with them. People like Ivor. But Trelawney—I can't fathom him. Would you believe he's never even tried to get me to go to bed with him? And let's face it, he wasn't like that in his early twenties, was he? At all events, I'm going to marry Ivor, and that's that.'

Ivor. Of course. So her first impression had been the right one ... 'But why did you get engaged to Trelawney?' Dale demanded.

Rebie shrugged. 'It just happened that way. All I meant to do when I came here, after Buff left, was to mess things up for Arnie. I flirted with Tree like mad, and I guess I went too far, because the next thing I knew he'd asked me to marry him. So I had either to desist or to say yes. And of course I said yes. It seemed a good idea at the time.'

'And now it doesn't,' Dale said ironically.

'No—but that's Ivor's fault. He promised to play along, but now he's being difficult. He just doesn't understand. He doesn't know Arnie like I do. We had a really ding-dong row when you were in the pool, and he says if I insist on staying here now Buff's coming back, then it's the finish.'

Dale was mystified. 'What on earth has Buff to do with it? I'm afraid I don't follow you.'

'No, because you have the idea she's keen on Murray. Maybe she does like him a lot, but can't you see, Daisy, he'd be second choice? That's the whole point. Buff's been in love with Trelawney for years and years. Don't you remember how she used to glow when she came home for hols and he was there? It probably would have all worked out too, but Arnie had her bluffed. She moved over here, and poor Buffie just gave in and resigned herself to the thought that he was Arnie's. I'm not so easily deterred, and at least I've proved that he can't be really crazy about Arnie.' Rebie drew a deep breath, shifted a little to get back into the shade that had shrunk as the sun climbed up the sky, and looked at Dale thoughtfully. 'I guess you think all this is one great big mess, Daisy, and you're looking so disapproving. But I'll explain to Buff—and I'll do absolutely anything to cut Arnoldine Bell down to size.

Well, anything except marry Trelawney, but Buff's going to do that.'

She sounded quite positive, but Dale had her doubts.

'You can't manipulate people like that,' she protested, mildly. 'Trelawney won't marry Buff just to suit you—just because she's there——'

'Want to bet?' Rebie shrugged. 'He doesn't have what you and I call a heart, Daisy. He's too much the tough cynical male. But the simple fact is that at this point in time he's ready to get married and father some offspring. If he wants heirs, he can't put it off for ever. And if I can —well—catch him, then so can Buff. So can Arnie, for that matter, she's getting on but she's not past the childbearing stage yet. So that's where you come in—playing gooseberry for all you're worth and keeping alive the fiction of our engagement. Just till Buff comes,' she went on cajolingly. 'It's not much to ask, and I'd never ask it except that Ivor's made it impossible for me to stay. He just doesn't understand.'

Dale didn't really understand either. Her opinion of Trelawney evidently differed from Rebie's. She couldn't see him being manoeuvred so easily. Yet somewhere at the back of her mind an insidious voice was whispering, 'He's ready to get married. If Buff can do it—if Arnie can do it —then why not Daisy Driscoll?' Daisy tried to close her ears to it. Would she want to marry Trelawney like that? Of course she wouldn't.

'No.'

She discovered she'd said the word aloud, and she was taken aback at Rebie's reaction.

'What? You mean you'll let the whole thing come apart after all I've done?' she exclaimed angrily. 'Oh well, why should *you* care if Arnoldine Bell reigns supreme over the whole of this cattle station? Over Kevin and Buff and the whole of the Vining family, come to that. *You* only come here once in a blue moon—when it suits you—to make use of us. Despite all my family did for you years ago. You're a rotten friend, that's all I can say, all you want is to please yourself and get back to this man in Rockhampton, whoever he is.' She jumped to her feet and glared down at Dale. 'You won't even sacrifice a few days of your time—just a few days. And don't tell me I should make the sacrifices—I'm not going to lose Ivor.' She turned away her hands to her face, and Dale wondered if she was crying, or pretending to cry. And if she should give in and agree to stay, though it was all so crazy.

But Rebie wasn't crying. As Dale too scrambled to her feet, she took her hands away from her face and then she was grinding her heel hard on something in the grass—grinding and grinding, while Dale watched her uncomprehending. Then she stooped and picked the something up—with a furious movement tossed it into the air in the direction of the palms.

Her lenses, of course. Her precious contact lenses.

'Now I *can't* stay. I'll have to go to Brisbane,' she bit out. 'If all you want is to please yourself I can't stop you—Arnie will eat Trelawney alive, it'll just be poor Buff's bad luck. But don't call yourself a friend!' She picked up her towel and flounced off, and Dale stood there, her mind in a turmoil. What a silly, pointless thing for Rebie to have done! But now she simply didn't know what to do. Rebie had given her far too much to digest all at once, and she was expected to make a snap decision. Uppermost in her mind was the fact that Rebie had never had any intention of marrying Trelawney. If she'd known that, she thought bitterly, she'd have been saved all those pangs of conscience when she discovered she was falling in love with him. Yet wasn't it a mercy there *had* been something to hold her back? She might so easily have done something she'd regret otherwise.

Now there was nothing to hold her back if she stayed. Loyalty no longer came into it. She could enter the Trelawney stakes if she chose.

She hadn't made a decision when, some minutes later, she went slowly back to the house. Of course she knew that the only sane thing to do was to get out, and Rebie would never be her friend again if she did that. On the other hand, if she stayed, how well was she going to hold the fort? Not very well at all, she admitted unhappily, and it all seemed sordid beyond words.

What on earth was she going to do?

On the homestead verandah, Rebie was in the middle of telling Arnoldine and Ivor a story, and Dale heard her saying, 'Daisy and I have searched and searched and looked and looked. And I only took them out because my eyes were sore while I was lying in the sun. But they've completely disappeared. Haven't they, Daisy?' She turned as Dale came on to the verandah, her towel around her shoulders. 'I'll just have to go to Brisbane—I'm as blind as a bat and I feel terrible. What a blessing you and Daisy hadn't left, Ivor. I can't drive a yard without my lenses.'

Ivor was looking pleased and so, Dale observed, was Arnoldine, who said practically, 'You'd better get your things packed straight away, Rebecca. Do you want any help? I'll explain to Trelawney—he'll understand that you had to go.'

'I don't need any help, thanks,' Rebie said offhandedly. 'And I've already asked Daisy to explain to Trelawney and to tell him I'll be back as soon as I can.'

Dale's lips parted on a gasp, and Arnie said sharply, 'Dale won't be here.'

'Yes, she will. Daisy's been a darling and agreed to stay

and finish the curtains,' Rebie said blithely. 'Who'd want sewing on their hands when they come back from a honeymoon? And there's nothing urgent for you to go back for, is there, Daisy?'

Dale shook her head. She felt angry with Rebie, but what else could she do now but accept? She couldn't flatly contradict and make a liar of Rebie.

With a murmured, 'Excuse me—I'll go and dress,' she walked round the verandah to her room. Her mind had been made up for her. She was staying. She hadn't seen Trelawney for the last time after all.

CHAPTER TEN

'ANY excuse,' Arnoldine said bitterly as she and Dale turned back to the house after Rebie and Ivor had driven away. 'Of course she intended to go all the time—she was always given to untruths and to thinking of no one but herself. She wants to eat her cake and have it, that's plain.'

Dale felt a flash of dislike for Arnie, talking to her this way about Rebie. She said deliberately, 'I wish you wouldn't say such things about Rebie. She and I are friends, you know. And she's going to Brisbane because she needs new contact lenses.'

'I'm afraid I'm not so easily fooled as you are, Dale.' They went on to the verandah out of the burning sunlight. 'I don't believe Rebecca lost her lenses at all.'

'But she did!' Dale exclaimed. 'Didn't you notice at lunch——'

'Oh gracious, what would be easier than removing her lenses? And why didn't you go too as you'd planned,' asked

Arnoldine, suddenly attacking Dale.

'You know why,' Dale stammered, taken aback. 'You heard. Rebie asked me to finish the curtains.'

'Then you're a silly girl to have agreed. Next thing the weather will break. You could be stranded here for weeks, and Rebecca is well aware of that. She'll have the perfect excuse for not coming back from Brisbane. She should never have chased after Trelawney the way she did. She's the one who should be looking after her father so that Elizabeth could stay here where she belongs. Instead, she literally threw herself into Trelawney's arms till there was nothing he could do but ask her to marry him. I could have predicted her behaviour, of course. She used to throw herself at him when she was barely thirteen. I saw it. It was disgusting. It's no wonder he decided to learn man-agement somewhere else ... Well, I don't know what you're going to do, but I'm going to take a swim now we have the place to ourselves.'

Arnoldine disappeared inside and Dale stood biting her lip. She was stupid to have stayed. If Arnoldine had bluffed Buff, she was going to have no trouble in bluffing her, too. It was going to be ghastly! Heaven knew what Trelawney would think when he came home and found her still there, and his fiancée gone. Arnoldine wasn't convinced by Rebie's story, and she'd probably plant doubts in Trelawney's mind too.

Well, she thought forlornly, she had better do some sew-ing—a futile occupation, since Rebie wasn't going to marry Trelawney after all. But perhaps it would keep her mind occupied. Already she was churned up at the thought of seeing Trelawney again.

She put in the afternoon fiddling about with the chintz, matching the patterns, and accomplishing little. Towards sundown, stormy clouds built up in the sky, towering up and up, growing bigger and bigger until it seemed to Dale that they must burst, so tense was the atmosphere; dark, brooding, full of water that they were going to spill somewhere. Meanwhile the air indoors was stifling and the light from the sky seemed to come thickly, through copper gauze. Dale knew the enervating effect this weather could have, what it could do to tempers and emotions. She knew too the release when the rain came—it was something that no one who hadn't experienced it could fully understand. She remembered the wild thrill she'd felt as a child when the rain poured down in torrents, drenching the earth, rising in steam. The sound of it on the roof at night—absolutely deafening. And she remembered waking in the morning to find the lagoon had flooded, and the water was rising up and up towards the house. Everyone was racing around helping to move all that was movable upstairs, out of reach of the flood waters. That was at Jackalass. The homestead here was never flooded, but the feeling of tension, of excitement was the same.

Drenched with perspiration, she went restlessly on to the verandah. The sky was full of screaming parrots and cockatoos, and leaving the house Dale walked slowly down to the lagoon. About a dozen pelicans were coming down to the water, slowly, majestically. She watched them lowering their drawn-back legs as they hit the water, watched the half clumsy, half graceful stretching and folding of their great wings. It was no wonder Trelawney loved this place. She stood among the trees, feeling the air so heavy it lay against her body like a huge oppressive presence, half inimical, half persuasive. Love me and I'll love you. Hate me and I'll crush you like an ant—without compunction. There were sudden tears in her eyes and she knew she was so wrought up that the least little thing would send her emotions into orbit.

She felt sheer shock when she saw Trelawney coming down to the water. She stared at him, her heart beats reaching an anxious crescendo, and then her mind seemed to break into fragments. Had he been to the house? Did he know Rebie had gone? Did he guess what it meant? And had Arnie told him *she* was still here?

When he caught sight of her he paused and stared, then strode on to stop not more than twenty inches from her palpitating body. His face was streaked with sweat and dust, and the lines at each side of his mouth were so deep he looked haggard. She looked back at him fully as he exclaimed, 'Daisy! What the hell are you doing here? Hasn't Ivor left yet?'

So he hadn't been to the house. He knew nothing, and it was all up to her to offer the explanations, to support the fiction of a happy fiancée unhappily called away because of a mishap—and leaving her faithful friend to carry on with the preparations for her married life to come.

She tensed herself before she could tell him, 'Oh yes, Ivor's gone. But I—I stayed.' She stopped. She simply couldn't go on from there—tell him about Rebie. The dramatic, almost threatening light that poured down from the sky made the man who stood so close to her look more than human, heroic even. She felt herself totally inadequate. There was nothing larger than life about her, in her blue shorts and her checked shirt, open as far down as was decent.

'For God's sake, why did you stay?' Trelawney had thrust his hands into his pockets and he spoke so roughly that she shrank within herself. 'Didn't I tell you I'd see you at the coast in January? Wasn't that enough?'

She looked back at him bewilderedly. Did he suspect she'd stayed because she couldn't bear to be away from him? Surely not—though it was terribly close to the truth, and she knew it now that he was here, and she couldn't keep her eyes off him. Despite everything she was already longing to be in his arms, to have him kissing her savagely—even if it meant nothing at all to him. It was like a drug. And now that Rebie had opted out, wasn't she at liberty to take and to return his kisses? Even to let him, if he wanted, make love to her? The thought had no sooner formed than she rejected it. As far as Trelawney knew, nothing had changed, but even apart from that, she didn't want his lovemaking. If Rebie were to be believed, he'd have no trouble in putting someone else in her place—Buff or Arnoldine, whichever one was the most persuasive. It could even be Daisy Driscoll, if she tried hard enough. But she wasn't going to try at all; she knew it now. She didn't want him on those conditions. She had to learn to live without him, to get this madness out of her system, and the way to do that was certainly not to throw herself into his arms.

She moved slightly away from him.

'I stayed because Rebie asked me to. Just until B—until she's back.'

'Until Rebie's back? Where's she gone?'

'She—she had to go to Brisbane. She lost her contact lenses,' she explained in a rush. 'So you see——'

Trelawney nodded. 'Sure I see,' he said thoughtfully, his eyes speculative.

Dale wasn't altogether sure that he did see. He looked, in fact, as disbelieving and sceptical as Arnie had looked.

'She's always been helpless without her glasses. When we were children——'

Her story was cut short before it could even begin by the sudden spilling of what seemed like thousands of gallons of water from the darkening sky. The birds were screeching, and Dale and Trelawney began to run for the garden and the house. It was exciting, exhilarating—like a visitation from heaven—and at last they stood gasping on the verandah, to discover Arnie there waiting for them.

Trelawney ran his hands over his drenched hair and a stream of water ran down his face, while Dale stood trying to catch her breath, her clothes clinging wetly to her body.

'You'd better get out of those things,' he remarked, his eyes running over her.

It was a reprieve. She turned away and went round the verandah to her room. She didn't want to be there when Arnoldine told her version of Rebie's departure.

In her room, she stripped off her drenched clothes and stood naked, listening to the mad rain thudding on the roof, smelling the wet earth and the slashed green leaves, feeling the heavy warmth of the room around her like a cloak, her body almost instantly dry. All the drama of the Wet came back into her mind nostalgically—the sounds, the scents, the colours. The tears and quarrels, the frayed tempers, the sudden streaks of humour that broke the tensions and cleared the air—— There was nothing like it and never had been. 'I love it,' she thought, senselessly because she knew very well that the Wet and its attendant discomforts lasted for months. All the same, she loved it—she was a fanatical devotee——

And she had better snap out of it and get into some clothes instead of standing here as though she were in a trance.

She put on the beige jeans and a clean shirt, then took some time combing her wet hair into shape. The rain stopped abruptly. There was silence, the air was steamy, beyond the verandah the night was purple-dark.

Dinner was for four. Thank heaven for Murray, Dale thought. Dining alone with Trelawney and Arnoldine would have been too nerve-racking for words. As it was, it was accepted outwardly at least that Rebie had taken off for Brisbane to get new contact lenses.

After dinner, Trelawney suggested a walk in the garden to escape the humidity indoors. The others approved of the idea, but Dale hung back. Trelawney paused near the two shallow steps.

'Coming, Daisy?'

Across the verandah their eyes met and Dale's pulses fluttered.

The rising of her emotions frightened her, and she said nervily, 'I haven't the energy. I'm going to bed.'

He gave her a long odd look, then with a brief, 'As you please,' went on to join the others.

Dale scarcely slept that night. Her mind went over and over the days ahead. How long would it be till Buff came? If there was more rain like they'd had tonight, Buff mightn't make it. And then she'd be stuck here. It wasn't as if her presence would do any good; she knew very well she couldn't stop anything that might happen between Trelawney and Arnie. Besides, as far as he knew, he was still engaged to Rebie. In other words, there was no point at all in her being here and she couldn't see why Rebie should think there was. It would be unbearable to be stranded here, the way she felt.

'I'll leave,' she thought, just before she fell asleep.

She woke to a burning brilliant day. Trelawney and the jackaroo had gone, presumably to begin mustering the flood-endangered paddock, so only Arnie was there to be told of her decision.

'Very wise,' said Arnoldine. 'If you don't go now you'll be stranded, and much as we love having guests, they're really not awfully welcome in the Wet. I suppose you'll stop by at Jackalass, though the others will have left for Brisbane, and Kevin will most likely be away from the homestead. Do you want me to ring through and find out?'

Dale shook her head. Arnie was right, there'd be no one there. Her departure, in fact, was going to be a very private one. She packed up once more and said goodbye to Mrs Miller, who persuaded her to have a sandwich before she left. She didn't write a note for Trelawney, she didn't trust herself.

'Say goodbye for me,' she told Arnie. 'I thanked him for everything the other day. I hope he won't think me bad-mannered for leaving so suddenly.'

'Oh, bad manners don't come into it,' Arnoldine reassured her. 'The rain last night was enough to frighten anyone away. I'm surprised Trelawney didn't suggest you should go himself, but he probably didn't want to hurt your feelings. Anyhow, you mustn't worry. He'll understand.'

She looked so pleased that Dale felt a qualm.

But honestly, she told herself when she was finally on her way—and without having left an address—what was the point in staying? And wasn't it only good sense to go while she could? If Buff *did* get there, then they could sort it all out without her help—Trelawney and Arnoldine and Buff. And Murray.

She heard herself give a despairing little laugh. Warathar was certainly no place for her, and Rebie would have to take it or leave it. She'd known Dale didn't want to stay.

She drove on.

When she reached the watercourse—that dry sandy bed of pink sand where a trickle of water had run when she came across from Jackalass with Trelawney—she put her foot hard on the brake and stared aghast. Water was racing down it now—brown boiling water, the colour of milk coffee. She sat and stared, her mind ticking over. It surely couldn't be very deep. She remembered dodging a few holes, a few boulders last time, but that was all. And this was certainly the regular crossing place—she could see wheel tracks on the far side of the stream.

Well, what was she waiting for?

She drew a deep breath, put her foot on the accelerator, and charged.

Great! The Torana entered the water with a splash of triumph, and the water surged up at each side. It was deeper than she had expected—and it was wider. But that, she realised suddenly, was because it was widening by the second—widening and deepening and becoming more turbulent. At almost the moment she realised this, her front wheel struck against something. The car rocketed up, bounced, and stopped dead. Dale revved the motor, hit the accelerator and leaned forward tensely in the seat. Nothing happened except that the Torana shuddered. Dale shuddered too. She tried to start the motor once more, and again without result. Then the boulder or whatever it was that had caused the trouble moved, and the Torana swung slowly round to the right till it was facing downstream, and Dale had an awful feeling that in a moment she was going to be afloat.

Oh God, it was unbelievable that in a few minutes so much water could have come down! She leaned from the window to look upstream, afraid of what she might see. She'd heard tales of flash floods—of the river coming down like a wall of water, sweeping everything ahead of it—trees, cattle—cars—— What if it should happen now? But there was no six-foot wall of brown flood water, though she could hear a distant roaring—and she could hear her own heart beating. It was no use trying to start the car. She couldn't control it and very soon, with the way the river was rising, she knew it was going to be swept away.

She'd have to get out.

She got the door open and leaving everything—even her handbag—she let her feet slide into the brown seething water. It seized on her at once with terrifying power, and she clung desperately to the door. What on earth was she to do? She'd never make it back to the bank she'd just left; the stretch of pink sand was disappearing before her eyes. Yet if she stayed in the car what was going to happen to her? As she clung there, her mind in a turmoil, the wall of water that she'd dreaded, but not quite believed in, despite that ominous roaring sound, descended on her like a greedy giant. It snatched her from the car, submerged her, carried her away. She fought blindly and helplessly till she could fight no more. She couldn't breathe, her lungs were full of water, and thud! some floating debris caught her a stunning blow on the back of the head. For a brief instant she visualised Trelawney's face and tried to say his name, then there was a tightness across her chest and black dark engulfed her ...

She came to at hazy intervals to hear the murmur of voices, to feel softness under her head, to feel pain. She didn't seem able to open her eyes and her mind was unintelligible chaos. She didn't remember the river, she didn't know where she was or what was happening to her. Her periods of semi-consciousness didn't last long enough for her to reach anything like lucidity.

'Swallow this,' she heard, and then there were times when her head ached so badly she felt herself weeping weakly before she slipped down into blissful oblivion again ...

She opened her eyes, actually opened them, and felt light pouring in. Mrs Miller was standing in front of the bed she was lying on. Dale moved her head, winced slightly, and tried to smile. She parted her lips to speak, but no sound came, and she wept instead, silently.

'There there, dear,' Mrs Miller soothed. 'You're all right. You're better today.'

Dale slept.

When she opened her eyes next time, no one was there. She was lying flat on her back and she stared around her. Her head didn't hurt, and everything was clear. She was at Warathar in the room that had been her room. The house was quiet and she thought it was afternoon—late afternoon, because of the colour of the light. A few big drops of rain thudded on the verandah roof, and she remembered the flooded river bed—her car—her—getaway. But she hadn't got away. She was back at Warathar.

She sat up. Her head didn't swim and her mind was functioning. It was sundown, but what day was it? Had it been yesterday that she'd driven away? Something told her it had been longer ago than that. Cautiously she slid her feet over the side of the bed. She felt terribly hungry. She'd get dressed. She found she was wearing pyjamas that were unfamiliar—sleeveless and blue with a V-neck. Were they Arnoldine's? And her clothes—all her clothes had been in the car. So she couldn't get dressed.

And who—who had saved her from drowning? She remembered seeing Trelawney's face—but it hadn't been real.

'Daisy?'

She heard Trelawney saying her name and all her composure went. She put her face in her hands and cried. She felt the mattress move as he sat down on the bed and put his arms around her, and she turned her head and wept on his chest.

When she stopped crying, she raised her face. 'Your rib belt——'

'I've learned to live without it. But not without you.'

Dale closed her eyes. He hadn't said that. Her mind was wandering again.

'I'm—hungry,' she said.

'My God, you can talk about your stomach when——'

'When what?' She raised her face and opened her eyes, simply because she wanted to look at him again.

'When I'm trying to tell you I love you.'

Dale wanted to cry. She was dreaming, of course, she had to be. She turned her face and pressed her nose against his chest. She smelt male, Trelawney smelt of sweat. And she could feel the beat of his heart. She wasn't dreaming.

'When is it?' she asked indistinctly.

'What the hell are you talking about, darling?'

'When did I go?'

'Four days ago.'

Four days! Then for four days she'd been blacked out. What had happened between then and now?

'How did I get here? I was sure I was going to drown——'

'I was afraid you were too. I'd come home at lunch time and found you'd left—I knew the river had come down——'

'Was it you who——'

'Fished you out of the water? Yes, that's right. You've been concussed. Mrs Miller's been looking after you.'

Mrs Miller, Dale noted. Why not Arnoldine?

'Are these Arnie's pyjamas?' she asked.

'No, you've had a change. They're Buff's.'

Her eyes widened. 'Is she here?'

'She got here yesterday. The river's gone down.'

'Then you know about Rebie,' she said slowly.

'Sure I know about Rebie. But what do you mean? *You* don't know about Rebie.'

'I do, she told me before she left. She was—ditching you. And Buff—Murray——' she floundered.

'Buff and Murray are crazy about each other,' he said almost soothingly. 'But not like I'm crazy about you—not like you're crazy about me.'

She bit her lip, frowning, thinking about Arnie. 'I'm not crazy about you. I was leaving.'

Trelawney turned her in his arms. 'Daisy, how well are you feeling?'

'Perfectly well,' she said huskily. 'But—lightheaded. I'm —hearing things. I'm hungry, I guess. My stomach feels empty.'

'To hell with your stomach. It's your heart I'm interested in. Listen—*why* were you going if you know it was all off between me and Rebie? And don't tell me you were going back to your old boy-friend when we feel the way we do about each other.'

'No.' He was looking at her and she was looking at him, and she could read all sorts of things in his eyes that made her wish she wasn't feeling so weak. But she was in his arms, and all those things Rebie had said about him being ready for marriage—about Arnie or Buff or just about anyone being able to grab him if they really wanted—they no longer made sense. She discarded them completely and told him simply, 'I didn't know you felt this way about me. And—Arnie was there. I couldn't—I thought—well, she'd be so right for you. In lots of ways,' she added after a moment.

'Daisy, there's only one woman who's right for me, and that's you. If you weren't in such a fragile state—and so preoccupied with your stomach as well—I'd prove it to you.'

'I'm not preoccupied with my stomach,' she said shakily, feeling her blood run infinitesimally faster. 'And I'm not in a fragile state.' She knew very well it was an invitation, and she sighed as his arms went round her and he drew her back with him on the bed. She clung to him as he kissed her lingeringly and passionately, their bodies close together, and presently he said against her lips, 'I'll take pity on you now I've proved my point. You are still fragile, Daisy, and I'm not going to be a brute. You'd better get back into bed and I'll ask Mrs Miller to bring you something to eat.'

She gave in, but held on to his hand as he rose.

'Trelawney, have you told Arnoldine about—us?'

'I didn't have to tell her. She knew when I brought you home from the river.'

'What will she do?' she asked hesitantly. She felt bad about Arnie.

'She's done what she's going to do. She left for Charters Towers yesterday after the river went down. She wants to look after David—she doesn't trust this housekeeper Buff's got hold of.'

Dale couldn't help it. She felt relieved, and it showed in her face as she asked him, 'Do you mind?'

Trelawney sat down on the bed again. 'Now look here, Daisy—if you're feeling even a twinge of jealousy, we'd better clear this up. In case you're wondering, I never made a pass at her since I left Jackalass years ago. That little affair ended then. But I like her, and I always have, and she was good to me when I badly needed someone after the affair of Stephanie. I'm glad she's gone to David; something will come of it and they'll both be happy. Rebie mightn't like it, but it will be the best thing for both her and David —he's only fifty-two, after all. He shouldn't spend the rest of his life alone. Arnie's always fitted into station life, and if David hadn't had a wife, she'd have fallen in love with

him when she came there as governess. I was just a sub-
stitute.'

Dale nodded, though she didn't believe it. It would be
terribly easy to fall in love with a man like Trelawney.

'Now what's bothering you?' he asked, touching the
little crease that had appeared between her eyebrows.

'She was here,' she faltered. 'In your house.'

'Where else was she to go?' he said reasonably. 'As a
matter of fact, I made an oblique suggestion she should
go to Charters Towers, but she didn't take the hint, and one
can't push these things. She has a very soft spot for this
part of the world, you know.'

Dale was far from sure that was why she hadn't taken
the hint, and though she didn't say so, he asked firmly,
'You're not going to bear a grudge, are you?'

'No,' she said quickly. After all, she was the one Trelawney loved—and what on earth was Rebie going to make
of that? she wondered. She said wryly, 'Rebie's going to
be surprised. She wanted to keep you in the family. She
thought you might marry Buff.'

'Oh, Rebie will get over it. She'll be full of her own
importance if she marries Ivor, which I suspect she means
to do. His old man's a land developer, and practically a
millionaire. You needn't worry about her.'

'It's funny that it's turned out this way, isn't it?' she
said. 'I mean, when I arrived at Jackalass that night and
there was just you there—I was terrified.'

'Were you? Why?'

'I thought you were so wild.'

'Darling, with you in my bed I'll never be wild again, I
promise you. Do you know I was rocked when I discovered how fanatically I'd fallen in love with you—and
there was I engaged, and you were all tied up in knots over

that guy you didn't go to bed with—thank heaven. I was determined to have you—that's why I asked you to come to Warathar and do some sewing. It was the only way I could hang on to you till I got free of my engagement.'

'But how did you know you would get free of it?' Dale asked.

He gave her a quizzical look. 'Rebie doesn't like the Gulf country. She'd have run a mile before she'd have let me take her within cooee of the altar. She didn't really want to get engaged to me, she merely meant to upset Arnoldine's applecart, and I knew it damned well. But she was very provocative, so I took advantage of it. I imagined Arnoldine would settle for Charters Towers once I was safely engaged, but she was too wise.'

Dale sighed. The room was almost completely dark now, and Trelawney reached across and switched on the bedside light.

'I'd better see about some sustenance for you, darling. Thank God you haven't broken any bones—I couldn't face a month of total abstinence.'

'I'll soon be back to normal,' she said, colouring faintly, and then as he rose to go, she said hesitantly, 'One other thing, Trelawney—I didn't tell tales about you to Uncle David—or even to Rebie. Maybe it doesn't matter to you, but it does to me, and I want you to know. I suppose it was Rebie—she must have been awake and heard you when you spoke to me.'

'That figures,' Trelawney agreed. 'She never liked Arnoldine, and probably thought she'd get rid of her ... So okay, darling, I agree that you're spotless. What a girl to have to live up to!' he added mockingly. 'I'm afraid you'll have to accept me as I am—sins, scars and all. I'm far from perfect.'

'Not to me,' Dale said huskily. 'I'm—I'm so mad about you I can't see straight.'

'I hope you keep feeling that way,' he said soberly, and leaned down to put his arms around her again.

Mills & Boon Classics

The very best of Mills & Boon
romances, brought back for those of
you who missed reading them
when they were first published.

In
June
we bring back the following four
great romantic titles.

ONE MAN'S HEART
by Mary Burchell

A harmless — well, fairly harmless — escapade took an
unexpected and horrifying turn that nearly landed Hilma in
serious trouble. But fortunately there was a handsome and
chivalrous stranger at hand to help her.

THE KISSES AND THE WINE
by Violet Winspear

Lise supposed she ought to be grateful to the imperious Conde
Leandro de Marcos Reyes for helping her out of an awkward
situation — but not so grateful that she was willing to repay
him as he suggested, by pretending to be his fiancée. A
domineering Spanish nobleman was not her idea of a comfortable husband. However, she reluctantly agreed to the
deception, just for a short time . . .

THE WATERFALLS OF THE MOON
by Anne Mather

'He's allergic to emotional entanglements,' Ruth declared after
she encountered the disturbing Patrick Hardy. But it was an
allergy that Ruth unfortunately didn't share and she tricked
Patrick into marriage and accompanied him to Venezuela.
Would her husband ever forgive the deception?

MAN IN CHARGE
by Lilian Peake

Juliet was delighted to get the job at Majors boutique, and full
of ideas and enthusiasm about it — but she found herself
continually in conflict with the man in charge, the chairman's
son, Drew Major. She wanted to keep the job — but was it
worth it, if it meant fighting this cynical man every step of
the way?

CUT OUT AND POST THIS PAGE TO RECEIVE

FREE
FULL COLOUR
Mills & Boon
CATALOGUE

and – if you wish – why not also ORDER NOW any (or all) of the favourite titles offered overleaf?

Because you've enjoyed *this* Mills & Boon romance so very much, you'll really *love* choosing more of your favourite romantic reading from the fascinating, sparkling full-colour pages of "Happy Reading" – the *complete* Mills & Boon catalogue. It not only lists ALL our current top-selling love stories, but it also brings you *advance news* of all our exciting NEW TITLES *plus* lots of super SPECIAL OFFERS! And it comes to you complete with a convenient, easy-to-use DIRECT DELIVERY Order Form.

Imagine! No more *waiting*! No more "sorry – sold out" disappointments! HURRY! Send for *your* FREE Catalogue NOW . . . and ensure a REGULAR supply of all your best-loved Mills & Boon romances this happy, carefree, DIRECT DELIVERY way! But why wait?

Why not – *at the same time* – ORDER NOW a few of the highly recommended titles listed, for your convenience, *overleaf?* It's so simple! Just tick *your* selection(s) on the back and complete the coupon below. Then post *this whole page* – with your remittance (including correct postage and packing) for speedy *by-return* despatch.

✳ POST TO : MILLS & BOON READER SERVICE, P.O. Box 236 Thornton Road, Croydon, Surrey CR9 3RU, England.
Please tick ☑ (as applicable) below:–

☐ Please send me the FREE Mills & Boon Catalogue

☐ As well as my FREE Catalogue please send me the title(s) I have ticked ☑ overleaf

I enclose £.............. (No C.O.D.) Please add 25p postage and packing for one book. 15p postage and packing per book for two to nine books (maximum 9 x 15p = £1.35). For TEN books or more FREE postage and packing.

Please write in BLOCK LETTERS below

NAME (Mrs./Miss)..

ADDRESS..

CITY/TOWN..

COUNTY/COUNTRY......................................POSTAL/ZIP CODE..............

✳ S. African and Rhodesian readers please write to: P.O. BOX 1872, JOHANNESBURG, 2000. S. AFRICA.

ORDER NOW FOR DIRECT DELIVERY

Choose from this selection of
Mills & Boon
FAVOURITES
ALL HIGHLY RECOMMENDED

☐ 1625
CALL OF THE HEATHEN
Anne Hampson

☐ 1626
THE THAWING OF MARA
Janet Dailey

☐ 1627
NIGHTINGALES
Mary Burchell

☐ 1628
DECEIT OF A PAGAN
Carole Mortimer

☐ 1629
STORM CENTRE
Charlotte Lamb

☐ 1630
DARLING DECEIVER
Daphne Clair

☐ 1631
PROMISE AT MIDNIGHT
Lilian Peake

☐ 1632
CLAWS OF A WILDCAT
Sue Peters

☐ 1633
LAST APRIL FAIR
Betty Neels

☐ 1634
TIGER SKY
Rose Elver

☐ 1635
PAGAN LOVER
Anne Hampson

☐ 1636
APOLLO'S DAUGHTER
Rebecca Stratton

☐ 1637
GARDEN OF THORNS
Sally Wentworth

☐ 1638
CRESCENDO
Charlotte Lamb

☐ 1639
BAY OF STARS
Robyn Donald

☐ 1640
MARRIAGE BY CAPTURE
Margaret Rome

☐ 1641
BINDABURRA OUTSTATION
Kerry Allyne

☐ 1642
KELLY'S MAN
Rosemary Carter

☐ 1643
DEBT OF DISHONOUR
Mary Wibberley

☐ 1644
DARK ENCOUNTER
Susanna Firth

ONLY 65p EACH

SIMPLY TICK ☑ YOUR SELECTION(S) ABOVE, THEN JUST COMPLETE AND POST THE ORDER FORM OVERLEAF ►

The Mills & Boon Rose is the Rose of Romance

Every month there are ten new titles to choose from — ten new stories about people falling in love, people you want to read about, people in exciting, far-away places. Choose Mills & Boon. It's your way of relaxing.

June's titles are:

JACINTHA POINT *by Elizabeth Graham*
To save her father, Laurel had been forced to marry the masterful Diego Ramirez, a man she did not know and certainly did not love.

FUGITIVE WIFE *by Sara Craven*
Briony had no doubts about her love for Logan Adair. Yet their marriage had been nothing but a farce from the very beginning.

A FROZEN FIRE *by Charlotte Lamb*
What would happen to Helen's sense of duty to her blatantly unfaithful husband now that Mark Eliot had come into her life?

TRADER'S CAY *by Rebecca Stratton*
There was bound to be tension between Francesca and Antonio Morales, but it was Francesca's relationship with his son Andrés that caused the real trouble between the two of them . . .

KISS OF A TYRANT *by Margaret Pargeter*
When Stacy Weldon first met Sloan Maddison he seemed decidedly antagonistic to her; yet why should he concern himself over the job his mother had offered her?

THE LAIRD OF LOCHARRUN *by Anne Hampson*
What had the formidable Craig Lamond been told about Lorna to make him so hostile to her?

NO WAY OUT *by Jane Donnelly*
Lucy's beloved twin sister had pretended to Daniel Stewart that she was in fact Lucy, and it shouldn't have been difficult for Lucy to deceive him in her turn. But . . .

THE ARRANGED MARRIAGE *by Flora Kidd*
Roselle's marriage to Léon Chauvigny had never been a real one. Now the time had come to end it once and for all. Or had it?

OUTBACK RUNAWAY *by Dorothy Cork*
Running away from the heartbreak of a disastrous love affair, all Dale found was Trelawney Saber, with a bracingly unsympathetic attitude to her troubles!

VALLEY OF THE HAWK *by Margaret Mayo*
Damon Courtney jumped to all the wrong conclusions about Corrie — and turned her life upside down in the process!

If you have difficulty in obtaining any of these books from your local paperback retailer, write to:

Mills & Boon Reader Service
P.O. Box 236, Thornton Road, Croydon, Surrey, CR9 3RU.